DEATH ON HER DOORSTEP

DEATH ON HER DOORSTEP

Sarah J. Mason

Chivers Press • Thorndike Press
Bath, England   Waterville, Maine USA

This Large Print edition is published by Chivers Press, England, and by Thorndike Press, USA.

Published in 2003 in the U.K. by arrangement with the author.

Published in 2003 in the U.S. by arrangement with Chivers Press Limited.

U.K. Hardcover   ISBN 0–7540–8835–9 (Chivers Large Print)
U.K. Softcover   ISBN 0–7540–8836–7 (Camden Large Print)
U.S. Softcover   ISBN 0–7862–4888–2 (Nightingale Series Edition)

The text of this Large Print edition is unabridged.
Other aspects of the book may vary from the original edition.

Set in 16 pt. New Times Roman.

Printed in Great Britain on acid-free paper.

British Library Cataloguing in Publication Data available

Library of Congress Control Number: 2002111997

AUTHOR'S NOTE

It is undeniable that both the University Boat Race and the Crime Writers' Association exist in fact. Readers will quickly guess how much of the rest of this book is fiction.

CHAPTER ONE

Josephine was waiting for her when Sally Jackson finally arrived home.

Or perhaps it would be more accurate to say that Miss Jackson had small doubt that it was Josephine whose yellow eyes, caught in the headlights, gleamed from the top of the gatepost as the weary crime writer turned the car cautiously into the still-unfamiliar drive. One black cat, whether exquisite Persian or short-haired moggy, looks much like another in the dark, when all that can really be seen of them is their eyes: but as far as the yawning Sally troubled to consider the matter there was no mistaking the accusing fluorescent glare of her feline acquaintance from the bungalow next door.

She wondered which had annoyed the little cat more. Was it the way she had sneaked off that morning without saying where she was going? Or was it the lateness of the hour at which she had condescended to come back? Miss Jackson mused (and not for the first time over the past three weeks) that the nature-not-nurture theorists might profit from taking a good long look at Josephine. Given her heredity, the cat seemed to have a surprisingly puritanical view of what most normal people would hardly call riotous living.

1

Sally braked the car in front of the garage and climbed out, stifling another yawn before bending to unlock the overhead door. As it groaned open she swung her torch back up the drive, to see that accusing yellow glare flash down from the gatepost and begin a slow, stately advance towards the house. By the time Miss Jackson had driven the car inside, switched off lights and engine, fitted the steering lock, collected her bag and seen that everything was secure for the night, Josephine had settled her dainty, fluffy self on the gravel by the front door step, her plumed tail lashing with obvious impatience, her yellow eyes narrowed and no hint of a purr from her normally welcoming throat.

'I'm tired, you know,' Sally reproached her as the beam of her torch found the keyhole. 'And I'm stone cold sober—two glasses of wine with supper, and ginger ale before and after because I knew I'd be driving. Does that meet with your ladyship's approval?'

Lazily, Josephine arched her back and yowled, making it clear she refused to believe a word Sally said. Or else all this talk of drinking had made her thirsty.

As was Sally. 'Would you like a splash of tea?' There was a clatter of keys, and the door opened. 'I'll be having a cup.' Sally reached inside to switch on the hall light. 'Or a chocolate biscuit? You had the last of the kipper yesterday . . .'

Sally had worried, at first, that offering to share (or being induced by those yellow eyes to share) the occasional snack with her might somehow alienate the affections of Mrs Manchester's cat: but the housebound old lady in the neighbouring bungalow had been only too delighted when Josephine found another willing slave. From the minute that elegant form in the magnificent sable coat had first padded across the lawn to investigate the smoked salmon sandwiches chosen by the newcomer for a housewarming treat, Sally Jackson had bought more fish than in the five years since her own little cat had been taken from her by a careless driver.

'. . . So, no kipper,' said Sally. 'Sorry. But— yes, do, please be my guest,' she told the plumy black tail as it disappeared along the hall towards the kitchen. Josephine had waited for no invitation but went prowling ahead before Sally finished speaking, waving her wild tail and walking her graceful lone, twitching her whiskers, and allowing the ghost of a friendly purr to rumble around Sally's ankles as she brushed past her hostess and crossed the threshold.

Miss Jackson grinned as she dropped her bag on the sturdy wooden hall chest beside the front door, to swap her driving glasses for those she wore around the house. Then she locked the door and, having glanced at her watch, chained it. Josephine clawed on the kitchen door, which stayed closed; she clawed more sharply with the other paw, and a screech of paint set Sally's teeth on edge. There was an irritable flick of Josephine's tail and she composed herself to wait, not even glancing over her shoulder as Sally's feet drew closer and she reached out to the door handle. Josephine stalked through the widening gap ahead of her hostess.

'It will take a few minutes,' apologised Sally. 'But—' she made for the fridge—'there's always milk while you wait.' Josephine gave her a sagacious yellow stare as she removed a bottle from the rack in the open door and bent to retrieve a saucer from the floor. 'Half a day's dust,' she observed, holding the saucer to one eye and tilting it to the light. 'Aha! Not a single footprint to be seen—no spiders, no mice, no bookworms. Thank you and well done, Josephine.' The tip of Josephine's tail gave an acquiescent twitch. 'The memory lingers on,' said Sally. 'Your reputation has certainly kept the villains away.'

Having rubbed the saucer ostentatiously on her jeans she held it under a running tap, twirled it for a moment or two, shook it dry and then dried it properly with a paper towel. 'Wait,' she reminded her little friend. 'Would you care for a crumb of digestive while the kettle boils?'

Josephine's whiskers twitched as she sniffed with annoyance at the empty saucer, now returned to its usual place. 'Not straight from the fridge,' said Sally, busying herself with taps and kettles. 'But it won't take long, and we can share a digestive while we wait . . .' She suppressed another grin. 'It's only plain, I'm afraid.'

It had been a defiant gesture on Sally's part to buy plain chocolate digestives this time around. Very early in their acquaintance Josephine had made known her preference for milk chocolate, but in the course of her most recent shopping trip Sally had deliberately bought the other kind. In five years she had developed a taste for freedom, and there were times now when she rebelled against being bossed about by something—someone, anthropomorphically speaking—who (or which) weighed no more than a few pounds, soaking wet. It was hard to adjust to these new feline chains, if only for a few weeks.

Josephine's ears flicked and her tail twitched as she recognised the sound of a tin being opened and heard the familiar rustle when Sally lifted out the packet and prepared to stab into it with a sharp knife. The little black cat yowled again, softly.

Sally stabbed; and for once the point of the blade went in with a crisp pop instead of a dull, mangling crackle. She rotated the cellophane cylinder on the worktop and the knife slid cleanly through. Sally smiled, pleased at her neatness when—smothering yet another

5

yawn—she really was rather tired. She took off her glasses and rubbed her eyes. Josephine yowled at her to hurry. The kettle bubbled its way to boiling point and automatically switched off as Sally tipped biscuits on a plate, broke one in half, and passed it down without a word to her imperious visitor.

Now warming the teapot, from the corner of her eye Sally watched Josephine sniff at the chocolate coating, recoil, and twitch her whiskers. The yellow eyes darkened to green, narrowed to slits. Was that a faint growl? The black bushy plume of her tail swept over the floor in an irritable arc, and she flicked her ears again.

'Sorry,' said Sally cheerfully. 'It's plain chocolate or nothing—but now you can have a drop of milk, if you'd like it.'

Having warmed the pot she dropped in a tea-bag, topped it up with boiling water, and set the timer for four minutes. She warmed the saucer with more hot water, and poured in just enough milk for Josephine to enjoy its flavour without having her taste-buds frozen.

This time, after a pause, there was a tiny purr. Not loud, not long; more a chirrup than a purr; but certainly a start. Sally, the chirrup suggested, might be forgiven. Josephine's eyes glinted as she looked up at her hostess with an air of distant approval; the lashing black plume was stilled as she wrapped her tail neatly around her paws, and purred with more enthusiasm.

'Friends?' Sally bent to tickle her under the chin. With a long, slow blink and another chirrup in her throat, Josephine signalled that she might indeed, if not mistreated further, be prepared to resume full and friendly relations.

But she continued to ignore the biscuit, which Sally kicked gently out of the way as she went back into the hall to take off her outdoor clothes. She slipped off her anorak, hung her cap on a peg, and sat on the bottom stair to unlace her driving shoes. Once she had swapped them for slippers the tea should be ready. She would coax Josephine out through the back door and potter upstairs, to read in bed while she enjoyed her tea and tried not to remember too much about the day's entertainment. True, it had been no more ghoulish and grisly than similar events—a good deal less grim, indeed, than some: but late at night, in a still-strange house, on her own, she felt she wanted no more of the wrong sort of image flashing upon her inward eye as she drifted at last off to sleep.

'Come to watch the floor show?' With her head high and her tail waving Josephine had stalked out of the kitchen, to sit precisely halfway down the hall in the exact middle of the floor, where she knew Sally would have to dodge round her whichever side she stepped. 'It's not very exciting,' said Sally.

She curled her toes tightly and relaxed

7

them, then rocked back and forth a few times on the balls of her feet. 'Aah, that feels better. Slippers—slippers . . .'

As she moved her shoes aside to reach for her slippers, the fluffy black statue that had been the seated Josephine decided to leap across the carpet to pounce on a trailing lace. Sally chuckled, then tweaked shoe and lace just out of reach. Josephine pounced again on her prey, smacking at the lace with first one paw, then the other, her claws making little scratching, snagging sounds on the drugget at the bottom of the stairs.

The chirping bleeps of the timer sounded from the kitchen. 'I've told you before,' said Sally, 'I hate stewed tea. The game's over.' She tried to push Josephine gently away, but the little cat made it plain that no, the game was not over. She smacked and scratched and snagged all the more at the now lifeless shoelace.

'No, Josephine,' said Sally. 'Enough, please. You've had your fun, and I want my tea. Stop it.'

Shoving her feet into her slippers she scooped up the cat and held her as she rose to her feet. Josephine grumbled once, softly, then drooped, completely motionless.

'Good girl,' Sally told her, and was about to make for the kitchen when she froze.

Josephine was in her arms. She wasn't moving.

Neither was Sally.

But that scratching, scrabbling sound hadn't stopped.

'Surely it can't be Mrs Manchester!' Josephine's owner, Sally knew, almost never left her bungalow. Crippled with arthritis, she could only move about indoors with the aid of elbow crutches or a walking frame; and even then she moved very, very slowly. And Sally knew that, had she managed to force herself outside at this time of night, she was so bent with age and pain there was no easy way she could reach the doorbell.

Unless it was an emergency.

'Something's wrong,' Sally said. 'She knew I was coming back late—she'll have guessed you'd drop in for a chat—she must be ill, and her phone's out of order.'

This was a possibility. Miss Jackson and Mrs Manchester lived on the very edge of the little seaside town: the house rented by Sally was the last along that road. From Sally's garden wall, trees and fields and empty, open spaces spread continually onward until they met the next town, seven miles away—open spaces over which the Channel winds often blew in a gusty fury, bringing down overhead cables, and fogging seaward windows with layers of airborne salt.

Sally was tired. She did not pause to reflect that if Mrs Manchester's phone was out of order, it was likely hers would have suffered

9

the same fate. Others might freely embrace the culture of the mobile telephone, but Sally had experimented with various models owned by friends and dismissed the tiny buttons and tinny acoustics as demanding far more patience and effort than she was willing to commit. She let Josephine spring from her arms and pad to the door, and hurried after her.

She unchained, unlocked, and opened the door. Light streamed from the hall into the blackness beyond, and caught a myriad flickering moths in its golden net.

There was nobody there.

With a yowl and a spitting hiss, Josephine sprang back. Sally looked down where she had been looking.

Sally did not move; she uttered no scream. She did not even gasp. All she could do, at first, was stare.

Stare at the ground. Stare at the step— across which was sprawled the figure of a man, face down, one arm flung forward in a groping gesture as he tried to reach the door.

A man in a dark jacket, across the back of which an even darker, sinister stain was creeping . . .

Sally cleared her throat and tried to stop her voice from shaking. 'Th-this isn't at all—at all funny,' she managed to bring out, after a couple of false starts. 'It—it's too hackneyed for words. Do stop being so s-silly.' She

10

stepped back. 'Please.'

There came no answer. No movement.

She edged forward, peering down, still not believing what she was starting, despite herself, to believe.

That groping hand groped once more, while the other dragged its painful way from under the sprawling body. With a snarl and one final hiss Josephine vanished backwards into the house, shaking her paws. Sally found herself throwing one envious look in the little cat's direction before, gritting her teeth, she moved stiffly across the threshold to the doorstep, where she hesitated, then knelt at the man's side.

She tried to turn him over. He was heavy. She tugged at his arms—his shoulders. Very heavy.

Almost a dead weight.

Almost dead.

'No! Not if I've got anything to do with it,' she told him in desperation, knowing even as she spoke there was very little her slight, unathletic, unmuscled five-foot-two in slippered feet could usefully do to help a helpless man at least twice her size. 'Don't try to move,' she urged breathlessly, taking her hands from his shoulders. 'I'll phone for an ambulance—fetch something for a bandage—'

Now the groping hand found a frantic strength and seized her by the ankle as Sally made to rise and move away. She shuddered, and despised herself for the instinctive recoil that made her try to break free even as a ghastly sound, a cross between a bark and a gurgle, burst from the man's mouth as he made a supreme effort, and wrenched his head round so that she could see his face.

So that she could read his lips.

He looked up at her, and muttered something.

And died.

CHAPTER TWO

Sally Jackson needed to attend only one meeting of the Crime Writers' Association before she was able to formulate the Golden Rule of Crime Writing: where two or more crime writers are gathered together they will socialise, with the intensity of the socialising being in direct proportion to the number of writers present. During her first annual CWA conference she and two new-found friends had spent so long chatting over after-dinner drinks in the hotel bar that the barman began slamming down the shutters in a very marked manner. But it had been twenty minutes past midnight: and (as another new friend remarked next morning at breakfast) even barmen go to bed. Which, nearby breakfasters agreed, would make a splendid title for a book: indeed, it sounded like a title even as she finished saying it. Now all Sally had to do was find the story to go with it.

From chatting with friends and colleagues Miss Jackson soon learned that she was one of the lucky ones. As over the years she became, in a very low-key way, successful, she accepted that for her it was not the finding of stories that was so much the trouble, as finding the time to write them. Others might need to be inspired wholeheartedly by An Idea before they could settle to work; many lost faith in the idea and stumbled at the dreaded Halfway Wall, where they were quite unable to pick themselves up and struggle on to the end. Sally tended to run into the wall two-thirds of the way through her first draft, yet so far it had never seriously blocked her path. When she came eventually to revise those tormented passages it was often difficult to remember where they had been, and it surprised her with each completed manuscript that none of what she had written was so very dreadful, after all.

Yet successful crime writing was more than just luck and a modest talent, a desk, an idea, and an adequate supply of paper: there was also the research, and it was the research that took up much of Sally's time. Before switching on her elderly word processor to type 'Chapter One' she might spend days, sometimes weeks, trying to understand enough for the purposes of her current fiction to make a plausible setting of oriental carpets, or Chinese art, or French gastronomy. Most of what she learned never appeared in the published book. Readers of mysteries have no wish to be bombarded with facts. Anyone requiring an encyclopaedia instead of a mystery will have bought an encyclopaedia in the first place; and the writer of fiction—of any genre—regards this as the iceberg effect, with five-sixths invisible under the water and the remainder riding easily above the waves as the story rolls as easily along.

But while a writer might use only one sixth in cold print, the effort is made with each book to have all six sixths as accurate as possible. Naturally, mistakes can slip through the most fine-meshed research net. Writers of fiction are not necessarily experts in what they write, and they are as human in error as any of their readers; yet a conscientious writer will strive to write with conviction, if not with authority. Sally's fellow members of CWA were of the same opinion; for which reason they tried to find to address and inform them people whose specialist knowledge was particularly relevant to the writing of crime and mystery fiction. Various guests over the years had spoken as fingerprint experts, as experts on police procedure, on ballistics, on unusual poisons . . .

The speaker at today's lunch engagement had been asked to address the topic of

Mistakes You Mustn't Make.

'I do hope,' Sally said, 'she doesn't bring any horrible slides.' She averted her gaze from the Bloody Mary being mixed for the writer just ahead in the drinks queue. There was something just then about generous helpings of tomato juice that somehow failed to appeal. 'Remember that full-frontal view of the shotgun victim last year?'

'And he said it got into the sequence by mistake.' Her companion snorted. 'A likely story. He wanted to watch us all squirm.'

'He succeeded—oh, what'll you have?' Mary was making her bloody way away from the bar, and the young man with the bow tie turned to Sally for her order.

'Ginger ale for me, please,' she told him. 'And . . .?'

'You bought them last time, but thanks. I'll have a gin and tonic. And don't let me miss my next round.'

'I won't,' promised Sally. 'And I warn you, if those slides are too grisly I'll be asking for a double brandy.'

In the event, she had no need. The official speaker-finder had obviously had a word in advance with Dr Sibyl Hedingham, warning her that though they might like to write—and to read—about gore, the members did not on the whole care to look at it. There had been occasions when people had passed out cold during talks with slide or film shows. One

15

member still bore a faint scar on his forehead from where he had bumped himself on the chair in front as he lurched into merciful unconsciousness before his neighbours had a chance to catch him.

Dr Hedingham began her talk and pleased her audience by announcing that her favourite reading was the crime novel, in all its different manifestations. Police procedural, thriller, old-fashioned cosy: she loved each and every one of them. But.

'But,' she went on, after this promising start, 'I'm sorry to tell you that I can't help losing a great deal of my willing suspension of disbelief, and my subsequent enjoyment of the story, whenever I come across anything that's an obvious mistake. I accept that it might only be obvious to me because of my medical knowledge: but it jars, nevertheless. It jerks me out of the fictional world you've gone to so much trouble to create for my benefit: and it's a great shame that sometimes I simply can't manage to make my way back into that world, because I'm forever worrying about what else might be wrong there that I don't have the expertise to judge. It niggles at me. False in one thing, false in all—though do please let me say,' hurriedly, 'that more recent books are much, much better than those written in what I understand you call the Golden Age.'

She smiled. 'No doubt it's the number of speakers you've asked to address you over the

16

years that has brought about such a noticeable improvement: in fact, from my knowledge of current crime fiction—and I include television programmes here—I'd say there's no real need for me to speak to you today, though of course I'm delighted to have been invited. It's honestly a thrill for me to meet so many people in whose company I have, as it were, spent so many happy hours in bed—and I hope you won't take that the wrong way,' as they all uttered the appropriate scandalised noises, and chuckled.

Dr Hedingham was an excellent speaker. She explained how wise it might or might not be to dissolve sleeping pills in whisky if the intended victim was not to spot them; she compared the efficiency of stabbing with a fencing foil to using a short vegetable knife; and she explained that it was far from easy to drown anyone in even moderate health unless they had been rendered more or less helpless first, which was more easily said than done. As for injecting anyone with a quick-acting and deadly bacterium, she could not in honesty advise it. The marks of an intravenous jab— the hasty pinprick (she insisted) simply would not do—remained visible long after death, and if the jabber played safe and had the body cremated he or she would need the agreement of not one, but two, criminally unobservant doctors to certify the corpse fit for disposal.

'As for do-it-yourself cremation,' they were

informed, 'it's not as simple as you might think. In the 1930s Alfred Rouse killed a tramp and left him in a blazing car filled with petrol, but the remains were still recognisably human after the fire was out—even though, in that case, the victim's identity was never established. Acid baths worked for Haigh, but they're awkward to arrange, unless you already have the facilities—and how many of us do? Your neighbours are bound to take notice if you suddenly start ordering carboys of vitriol, and they'll wonder why you want it. Much better have the death look like an accident: but even an accident isn't easy to arrange. You might think that dropping an electric fire in your victim's bath will do the trick, but you'd be amazed how few people really have been successfully killed in that way . . .'

The slides were mostly acceptable, although once or twice Sally blinked and took extra pains over her notes to avoid looking too closely at the screen. But Dr Hedingham seemed to know how far she could go without losing the sympathy of her audience.

She reached the end of her prepared talk and was loudly applauded as she extinguished the projector on the vivid image of a clinical thermometer side by side with the larger laboratory-style version used to determine the temperature of a dead body. 'And whatever else you do, don't have your police doctor pop it in the corpse's armpit . . .'

18

Question time came next. Someone wanted clarification on the diagnostic accuracy of rigor mortis; somebody else showed what many regarded as excessive enthusiasm, so soon after lunch, for the use of maggot infestation as a determinator for the time of death should the corpse of an undernourished female remain unburied in deciduous woodland on clay soil during a prolonged drought.

And it was while some of the audience, including Sally, still squirmed at the detailed answer that a voice from the back enquired:

'But how often is death truly instantaneous? I mean, how likely is it that somebody on the point of dying could survive just long enough to stagger across the hero's threshold and deliver the cryptic message that's the basis for the entire book?'

Dr Hedingham rubbed her nose, and frowned. 'That's a tricky one,' she said cheerfully. 'To be honest, I have to say it all depends on how your dying messenger was killed in the first place. You'd be surprised at how long someone can keep going when they've been stabbed, for example, or bashed on the head—unless it's a stab straight to the heart, of course, but they'd be really unlucky to have that happen—or an eggshell skull. Your knife will bounce off their ribs more often than not . . .'

An enjoyable meeting was prolonged by the majority of the group at last escorting their

19

guest to an equally enjoyable supper, where Sally's table began to argue the merits of the Dying Message as a plot device. There were those who considered it far too old-fashioned; they would accept that in certain circumstances it was physically possible, but they could no longer accept the cliché it had become. Others held it to be admissible simply because it was a cliché, except that they preferred the term convention. You knew (they insisted) where you were, with Dying Words. Really, it was impossible to lose. If the reader worked out what the words meant before anyone else in the book, it could only add to the pleasure of reading to be one up on the protagonist all the way through—always assuming, of course, that the mystery itself was fair. Which in the present company went without saying. If, on the other hand, the puzzle remained unsolved by anyone at all until the final pages, leaving the reader wide-eyed with admiration as the book was reluctantly closed, then that was only to be expected. The plot had worked out as it should, in the best tradition of the mystery. Or convention. Or cliché.

'What do you think, Sally? You're keeping very quiet at that end of the table.'

She hesitated before replying. 'I'm not sure,' she said at last. 'I think, but I wouldn't swear to it, I think I'd rather play safe and save the dying message plot for a last resort. I'm not sure I could invent anything cryptic enough to sustain a whole book.' Then she chuckled. 'But if by any chance I could, then believe me I would. Just once, for the fun of it. Because if we don't find our books fun while we're writing them, how on earth can we expect readers to have fun reading them?'

And there came a smattering of applause from around the table at her words, as with an approving hand her neighbour topped up her wineglass from the communal bottle, and the talk drifted off in another direction.

Even Sally thought no more about it.

CHAPTER THREE

Supper had progressed amiably to its conclusion and beyond, with further swapping of professional gossip over second and third coffee refills. Everyone enjoyed themselves so much that Sally was not the only one to lose track of the time, but a sudden concerted rush for buses, tubes and taxis saw them all safely if belatedly on their way.

Sally crossed London as springtime dusk turned finally to night, and arrived at Waterling Cross main line terminus in time to catch the last train but one of the day on the quiet local line. At Stourhaven she was the only passenger to leave the train, which rattled

21

off into the darkness with a mournful whistle. As it disappeared she made her way along the platform between pools of anaemic light cast by those lamps that had not yet been vandalised. Apart from Sally the station was, or at least seemed, uninhabited: the British Rail staff—Miss Jackson was impatient of trying to remember whatever new name they might choose to adopt this year—had clocked off hours ago. Apart from Sally, walking briskly out through the empty booking-hall with her sturdy torch in one hand and her car keys in the other, the only obvious movement was the swirl of a wayward crisp packet, caught in the slipstream as the train chugged away. The station lights lured no flickering moths; no owls drifted in search of prey, no pigeons scuttered after crumbs of crisp or biscuit, no cats prowled. Sally walked on, alone.

Even Rob Halliday, the temperamental taxi driver notorious for the strange hours he chose to keep, had gone home, or had never been on duty in the first place. His absence did not disconcert Sally, who that morning had parked as close to the main building as she could when commuters' cars took up most of the space available.

Inside the building all the lights had been switched off, in the concourse as well as the booking office. Passengers must rely on platform and car park lamps. It was a pity so many of these were dark. British Rail economy protects the solitary traveller, mused Sally. Or vandals, a sense of justice made her add as, with her torch firmly held and her glance alert, she headed for the solitary car more than halfway down the car park. She had thought her luck too good to be true when she found a bay within sight of a closed circuit t.v. camera; she had been right. At some time during the past few hours the nearest lamp had been broken, its glass glittering in the beam of her torch and, despite a wary detour, the odd sliver crunching under her feet. But no villains lurked behind litter-bins or lamp posts, and Sally reached her car in safety.

She checked over her shoulder before bending to flash the torch first under the car and then into the back seat. She opened the driver's door and hurried to settle herself with central locking and seat belt before starting the engine. As the headlights stabbed into the night and guided her to the main road, she found herself sighing with relief. While independence of mind and action were indeed very fine in theory, there were times when independence ranked a poor second against the convenience of being met by a taxi, except that what little she had heard of Rob Halliday's reliability had not encouraged her to think of booking the services of this eccentric one-man business in advance.

Josephine was waiting for her as Sally Jackson finally arrived home. After the solitary trip from London there was a decided comfort in having someone to talk to, even someone who didn't answer back—at least, not in words . . .

And now she was talking to someone else, who should have been able to answer her. It would have been a comfort if any answer—a cough, a gasp, a gurgle—had come: but the man on the doorstep made no answer as she peered into his face and tried to coax him to speak again.

She did not want to allow herself to express, even in her thoughts, the suspicion that he might be—

Perhaps he was not—

Dead.

'No!' She tried shaking him again by the shoulders. He might perhaps only have fainted. Sally was not medically qualified. Who was she to say that anyone was . . . dead?

Yet that gurgle had sounded horribly final.

And even when she shook him he did not move.

But her imagination had always gone into overdrive at the slightest thing—

Medically qualified.

Dr Sibyl Hedingham. The lecture that afternoon—

'Right,' said Sally with a gulp. 'That—that's it. I c-can't help it. I'm a coward.' She forced herself to lay the man's head, heavy as it was in her shaking hands, gently on the mat; then she staggered up and back into the house, closing the door firmly on the man outside, whether he was dead or alive. As the snib clicked she took a deep breath and felt her legs turn to jelly. It might seem callous, but she put up the chain and took another deep breath as she forced herself out of the hall to the sitting room, without turning on the light. Round the edge of the curtain she peered into the darkness.

Nothing moved. Nobody was watching.

She hoped.

She glanced sideways to the steps, illuminated by the warm glow of the hall light through frosted glass, and by the fainter glow from the street lamp nearby.

Nothing moved. The man lay just as she had left him . . .

She wasted no more time. She went back to the hall and the telephone, and—somehow—dialled nine-nine-nine.

*   *   *

The tea must be thoroughly stewed, she knew, but Sally found her hands shook far too much to risk filling the kettle and playing about with boiling water, no matter how cold she was starting to feel. Besides, she had little confidence in her ability to hold even a mug. Her hands shook quite as much as her legs. She felt sick. She sat down on the kitchen stool and tried to take several more deep breaths, in and out. Out, for an asthmatic, was more important. In, out—out . . . in, out—out . . . counting to ten each time she breathed. Was this, she wondered, time for an extra puff?

But her wondering was somehow . . . out of focus. Whatever had happened—might still happen—did not seem real, for all her nausea and shaking hands. She held out her hands. Shaking. Shaken. Shock. That was why she felt so cold and giddy and out of focus, why her heart fluttered and thumped by turns. Puffing at her inhaler would, she knew, make the shaking more pronounced. For shock, didn't people take a stiff peg of whisky or a slosh of brandy?

She decided against handling glass bottles. She would sit and breathe, and try to calm herself.

Josephine appeared from some corner or other, hissing. The fur bristled all the way down her spine, her tail was enormous, her eyes were slits.

'It's—it's all right, Josephine . . .'

Sally had not convinced the little cat, any more than she had convinced herself. Josephine inflated herself still further, spat, and raked her claws on the mat by the back door.

'Don't,' came the murmur as Sally shook her head: a shake that this time was deliberate, not nervous. Perhaps she was starting to

26

convince herself after all.

Perhaps. She hoped so. How long would it take for the emergency services to arrive from wherever they were based? She had not been living in Stourhaven long enough to know the topography of the place: she had taken an exploratory stroll on her first weekend in residence; had found the shops, the library, the doctor, the dentist; and the next Monday had gone straight back to work on her latest book. Publishers' deadlines did not wait.

Her publishers would never believe this. She glanced at the clock: no, even in New York the working day was long over. 'Fool,' she scolded herself. But was the initial shock fading as her brain began to work? She tried to rise from the stool, wobbled, and tried not to push her luck. She flopped back down. A friendly human voice just then would have been welcome beyond belief. Too late, or else too early, to ring anyone in London even if she could bring herself to dial. Her publishers would never believe this—

Publishers' *dead*lines—

She shut off that thought before it went another syllable—forced one more deep, double breath—and then made herself stand, count slowly to ten, and walk to the kitchen door. As she passed the packet of digestive biscuits her hand shot out—yes, it was shaking rather less now—and grabbed the knife as the other, fumbling—but of course it would fumble, it was her left, Sally was right-handed—fumbling, reached for the key, and turned it, and opened the door. Just wide enough, and no wider.

In a burst of angry fur Josephine was gone. And on the breeze Sally heard, to her relief, the sound of cars arriving somewhere near; and she saw, reflected over the roof of her house, shining on the windows of the bungalow next door, the electric blue pulsation of a police car's light.

* * *

Superintendent Groby could perhaps have been more immediately sympathetic. It was not just that he was tall and bulky, and loomed over Sally: most adult males loomed over Sally. She could hardly expect them to crick their necks and bend their knees on a permanent basis whenever she was in mixed company, and she did not. Height (or less than five foot three inches of it) was a fact of life as far as she was concerned. If the Lord had meant her to be seven inches taller, He would never have invented library steps.

Groby, however, loomed in what Sally could only describe to herself in her still-shocked state as the wrong way. His eyebrows were black, and twice as bushy as any eyebrows had a right to be. They met in an apparently permanent scowl over dark, deep-set, suspicious eyes. Somehow he made her feel she and no-one else was to blame for the presence of a dead man on her doorstep. If she had been an Amazon rather than the youngest wren of nine, she could have dragged the body indoors, restored him to health, and sent him on his way without having to bother anybody else . . . Particularly without bothering Superintendent Groby of Stourhaven CID, who had more than enough work on his plate without Sally's inadequacies adding to his woes.

A small voice from the better part of her nature tried to suggest that this scowling brusqueness could be Groby's way of jolting people out of whatever self-indulgent shock they might have allowed themselves to succumb to: yet Sally did not believe she was any more self-indulgent than the next person. And was not sure she believed the voice, either.

Perhaps it was because they had started badly.

Once the first flurry of explanation was over Sally had been delighted to leave the authorities to carry on with the routine of investigation at the front of the house. Followed by Superintendent Groby, she went back to the kitchen and began making another pot of tea, double strength.

'Sugar?' People normally had to ask for it; except in cooking she did not use it; but vague

29

memories of Girl Guide training prompted her to hunt out the canister and shake a few spoonfuls into a saucer. Groby's bushy brows signalled their disapproval by arching sharply upwards.

'I suppose there's a proper basin about the place,' she found herself apologising, 'but goodness knows where. I only rent this house, you see.'

'I see.' He sighed. 'No sugar for me, thanks. How long have you been staying here?'

'Three weeks.' She wondered how much he really wanted to know. 'I'm house-sitting while the owners are abroad.'

'Ah.' He nodded. 'Away for long, are they?'

'A year.'

The look on Groby's face was fleeting, but expressive. He was stuck with Sally Jackson in his manor for a further eleven months and one week. And if she had started out as she meant to go on, it was going to feel like a hundred and eleven months before she left.

'Friends of yours, Mrs Jackson, or did you hear about this place through an agency?'

Had she not at that moment been stirring the tea, Sally would have collected her thoughts before answering. But the timer had just rung—which made Groby jump, so that he shot her another black and bristly glare—and she spoke without thinking.

'Miss,' she said, with the spoon in one hand and the lid of the teapot in the other. Her left.

The hand with the plain gold band and the engagement ring on the third finger.

The glare shifted pointedly to the rings, and the black bristles arched. 'Divorced,' said the superintendent.

It was not a question. It was a logical deduction: he was, after all, a detective.

On a less fraught occasion Sally would have remembered that there are ways, and ways, of pointing out mistakes (no matter how logical) made by anyone. Especially by anyone whose job it is to make logical deductions. But . . .

'Married,' she corrected him without thinking. 'But I never changed my name. I mean I use it,' as another pointed glare came her way, 'for—'

Then she realised where this was heading; and it was too late to do anything about it. 'For—well, for professional purposes.'

The dark eyes skimmed over Sally's small frame and seemed to focus on the spectacles and the fine, mid-mouse hair. 'Actress?' She could not tell if his tone implied disbelief or sarcasm.

'Author.' Defiantly, she sipped her tea, bracing herself for what she knew he would ask before much longer.

'Author.' The superintendent jiggled his mug and scowled at the ripples dancing under the light. 'I won't ask if you write under your own name, of course.' Of course. One of the first lessons any writer learns. 'But ought I to have heard of you?'

Could she try telling him she wrote romantic fiction? No, he seemed too shrewd to fall for the six-a-year-with-as-many-pseudonyms line.

She was growing expert at taking deep, bracing breaths. 'Not unless you enjoy mysteries.' She could not look at him. 'Detective stories. That's what I write . . .'

Sally had come to crime fiction by the same route so many of her colleagues had followed. They knew they wanted to write, they knew they loved to read; it was logical that what they wrote should be the type of book they liked best. There could hardly be a better reason.

Readers might still find the first Sally M. Jackson on the library shelves, though it had been out of print for years. At the time of writing she had contrived for her firstborn the whimsical device that every character who appeared (except one) in the book bore the name of a character from Shakespeare, none of these characters having any physical Shakespearean presence. They were no more than a passing mention by someone whose name was in the cast list, and Sally found great amusement in fitting the sometimes quirky names (Pickbone, Nightwork, Shortcake) to those who bore them: a doctor, a nurse, a cook. She had thoroughly enjoyed the fun of creating this whimsy, and was lucky enough to find a kindly editor who not only found it fun but who chose to publish it. It was a regret to them both that most readers and reviewers failed to spot the Shakespeare joke, the rare exceptions being countable on the fingers of Sally's left hand. And none of them critics. This was par for the course, she soon learned. The book sank virtually without trace . . .

But by the time its last, weak bubbles had struggled to the surface she had discovered Mrs Beeton.

CHAPTER FOUR

Mrs Beeton was Sally's series character. A middle-aged widow, she had once been a cookery teacher who, on the death of her husband, took up her former profession again until she retired in a blaze of glory, having unmasked a murderer in such time as she had free from coaching her entire class to Grade One standard, with multiple Distinctions. As a retirement gift her colleagues had presented her with a genuine first edition of the celebrated volume on Cookery and Household Management written by her nineteenth-century predecessor and namesake.

Her admiring pupils clubbed together to give her a far more unusual token of their esteem: a gold-plated ladle, guaranteed non-polluting. Mrs Beeton, overwhelmed by this tribute, promised that she would use it wherever she went: and Sally saw to it that in her new profession of travelling cook-housekeeper she went to a good many places. It was noteworthy that, no matter where she might go, before too long someone would be murdered, and Mrs Beeton's knowledge of human nature would invariably help to solve the crime. The dénouement frequently occurred over dinner, often while the soup was being served. The way to a man's heart, Mrs Beeton maintained—it was her catchphrase, which she uttered at least once in every case— was through his stomach. Who better, therefore, to know the innermost secrets of a household than the household cook?

What writer understands how and why a series character can take hold and become almost real? In Sally's case she was completely bewildered. Her own culinary skills were basic in the extreme: a pot of tea, fingers of toast, a boiled egg, and blessings on the microwave oven and the supermarket cook-chill cabinet. In contrast Mrs Beeton—with the moral support of her gold ladle and her first edition—would whip up seven-course dinners at fifteen minutes' notice during the most desperate of crises. On a good day she could excel herself.

Yet Sally did not feel too intimidated by Mrs Beeton. Indeed she was fond of the talented crime-solving cook, and seldom needed to remind herself that few people possessed all the talents in equal degree. Mrs Beeton probably could not write; if she could, she had so far shown no sign of doing much more than scribble a note to a friend, or a list of ingredients. Sally's publishers had dropped one or two hints about a new 'Mrs Beeton' cookery book, and she suspected it was only concerns about copyright that had stopped them making a definite proposition.

If they did decide to go ahead it would be hard on Sally M. Jackson. Following a simple recipe was hard enough when timing and coordination played so vital a role in getting an entire meal to the table in the correct order. Having to forego recipe books and invent from scratch, and keep testing and tasting as invention demanded . . .

In part it was these inventive demands that had brought Sally to Stourhaven. She hoped the sea breezes might be good for her, after a damp winter and an unusually severe bout of bronchitis; and long, bracing walks along the seashore might ease the burgeoning chronic dyspepsia for which Mrs Beeton and Sally's uneasy conscience were equally to blame. During each of her adventures Mrs Beeton not only had to speak her catchphrase and hit someone over the head with her gold-plated ladle; she had also to cook.

And Sally's publishers preferred her to cook something different each time. Aware of their author's limitations they would supply her with recipes when she asked, and she herself scoured charity shops and jumble sales for unusual or out-of-print books. She felt, however, a strong moral obligation to try out in person any recipes used by Mrs Beeton, so that she could reply to any queries in those fan letters that might make it through the publishers' labyrinthine postal system to her home address. And for someone with a naturally small appetite too much rich food— even in half portions, and in a good cause— was bound to have its inconvenient side . . .

She shuddered now as she sipped her sugar-sickly tea. Shock or no shock, she could drink no more. There was enough over in the pot to give her an honest, unsweetened cup if she topped it up from the kettle. She glanced at Groby, and found him regarding her with a pained expression in those dark, suspicious eyes.

'Detective stories,' he said grimly, just as Sally asked:

'Would you like another cup of tea?'

He jiggled his mug again: it was still half-full. 'Not for me, thanks. But you go ahead.' The eyebrows bristled again as he watched her pour almost a whole mugfull down the sink. Wilful waste means woeful want: she could almost hear him thinking it.

'Pay well, do they?' he enquired. 'Detective stories, I mean. Can't say I read them myself, though the wife sometimes gets an Agatha

Christie out of the library.'

It was the old familiar story. Sally thanked heaven for Public Lending Right. 'Well, it helps to keep the wolf from the door—'

Something like compassion gleamed briefly in his eyes as he saw her shudder at what she had said. 'You'd like to do better, I dare say.'

'Wouldn't we all? But I've been luckier than many of my friends. It's taken years, but now I can just about afford to write full time.'

'Ha.' He glared into his mug of tea, which he had not yet finished. 'Talking of luck, you'll be able to make something of all this, will you? Boost your sales with the publicity? It'd make a good headline. The Corpse on the Doorstep. The Man on the Mat.'

Now it was Sally's turn to bristle. 'That,' she said, 'is one of the most—most monstrous suggestions I've heard for a very long time. As if I'd dream of—of cashing in on anything so—'

Then she choked. Surely he couldn't be suggesting—?

'And if you—if you imagine,' she went on, 'that I—I lured that poor man to this house just so that I could stab him to—to puff my books—'

'Now, how do you know he was stabbed?' Groby put down the tea he had no intention of drinking, and leaned—loomed—forwards. 'We haven't found a weapon.' His eyes seemed to bore through Sally to the worktop near the

37

door, where she had left the kitchen knife after letting Josephine out of the house.

'His coat—his coat was torn. Cut.' Now she had been jolted out of her trance it surprised her how much she had, without realising, noticed. 'It was . . . clean. Oh, there was blood, but it wasn't muddy, or frayed as if he'd caught it on a branch, or been hit by a car and dragged along the road, or anything like that. And a bullet-hole . . . well, I'd have thought it would be more—more noticeable, somehow, especially if it was the exit wound. Bigger. Rounder. Besides, if he'd been shot, he would have died . . . I mean, he wouldn't have lived . . .'

She stopped. She remembered that this was real life—real death—she was discussing, not one of the problems posed by an enthusiastic lecturer to an equally enthusiastic audience of crime writers.

Groby supplied the brutal conclusion to her theorising. 'He would have died quicker than he did? He'd never have lasted long enough to turn up on your doorstep?' He saw her shudder again, and went on:

'But it's not your doorstep, is it? Or only for the last three weeks, you say. Ha. Just how well do you know the owners of this house?'

'They're colleagues of—that is, the husband works with my husband. They're both in the petroleum industry. My husband's a sort of engineering troubleshooter. There's a good deal of Far East activity at the moment, and a couple of postings came up. One for a year at least, and another for three or four months. I'm not a good traveller,' she explained. Those black eyebrows made her feel defensive. 'And it didn't seem sensible to disrupt my work schedule for such a short time, with people never being sure where to find me—I have manuscripts and proofs and publicity handouts to check, and the couriers . . .'

That unhappy reference to publicity silenced her again. Groby sighed, then said—almost as if he really wanted to know, 'What about your own place? Left it empty, have you? A bit risky, these days. Squatters.'

'An American colleague is staying there for a while. A colleague of mine,' she added, before he could ask.

As if he had needed to. His glance clearly showed that he had already accepted the inevitability of the crime writing connection: he might disapprove of it, but he knew he was stuck with it. 'Not around these parts, I dare say,' he said.

'The other side of London. Hertfordshire.'

'Ha.' The look he turned on Sally now was another of those where something that might be compassion lurked at the back of his eyes. 'So you've no friends locally?' Was he asking for character witnesses? 'You don't know anyone who could pop in and keep you company for a while?'

Someone who could vouch for her? Or someone who could keep watch to ensure she did not flee the country on a fishing boat? Sally's reputation would be shot to pieces if her search for fresh air and exercise took her anywhere near the harbour before the case was solved.

'We could spare a female officer, if you'd like one.' Suddenly, he grinned at Sally: there might be a hint of sadism in the teeth, but to her amazement she realised that his intention all along had been, if not kindly, then certainly not as hostile as she felt he had been before. 'If you'd like one,' he repeated. 'Of course, there's no obligation.' Would a refusal seem more, or less, suspicious to those watchful black eyes? 'But you strike me as a lady who'd rather be independent than otherwise.'

Sally blinked. She blinked again, and cleared her throat twice before replying. 'Yes—yes, I think I would prefer to be left alone for the moment, thank you. I could do with a little peace and quiet.'

'Ha. Can't promise peace and quiet, I'm afraid. It'll take us more than a few minutes to finish up outside.' He grimaced. 'Give the neighbours something to chatter about, though. They'll be on the phone inviting you for coffee before you know where you are.' The eyebrows arched again as she opened her mouth to protest that she had spoken to only one of her neighbours during her entire three

40

weeks in Stourhaven. 'And they won't be the only ones, will they?'

Sally was puzzled. 'Won't they?'

'Reporters,' said—or rather snarled—Superintendent Groby. 'You'll be used to interviews, I dare say.' He made it sound like a crime. 'So long as you give us your statement first, there's nothing I can do to stop you. This is a free country.'

'I don't want to talk to any reporters,' she said quickly. 'I don't think I want to talk to anyone! If I don't talk about it, maybe it will make it less . . . real. Easier to forget—although . . .'

Groby rose to his feet and favoured her with a quizzical look. 'You're not to go forgetting before you've given us your statement, thank you,' he said. 'Some time tomorrow—but don't rush,' as she glanced automatically at her watch. 'You've given me the basics to be going on with, and we'll be pretty busy with the routine for a few hours yet. Once you've had some sleep and a bite to eat'll be time enough.'

He grinned a sharp-toothed grin. 'I think you'll find things look different in daylight, Miss Jackson. And if you do decide to talk about it before you've talked to us . . .'

This time she didn't even start to protest. He was the expert, she the innocent bystander. She had a feeling he might have the right approach.

'. . . Well,' he went on, 'you might try turning

your talk to our advantage. Clear the air. Work out what he was trying to tell you when he died.' He gave her another grin. 'Get your ideas sorted out—they're too muddled right now from the shock. Unless, by any chance, it's come back to you already—though you would have told me if it'd made any more sense, wouldn't you?'

'Of course. But . . .' She shook her head. 'I'm sorry, I can't say any more than I told you when you first arrived. He—he shouted at me, or at least he tried to, not to fetch an ambulance . . . said something about the harbour, and the sea . . .' Sally frowned. Yes, the superintendent had been right to suppose that talking about it might help to clear her muddled thoughts. 'The sea . . . and . . .'

He sat down again and waited, without speaking.

'The sea,' she reiterated. 'Yes. And—and something else that made me wonder about—about . . . poison.'

She felt herself grow hot as she saw him doing his best not to sneer at this evidence of the mystery writer's imagination in overdrive. 'Yes, I know it sounds silly, but I could swear he said he'd—eaten something . . . fish, could it have been? But . . .'

'Fish.' Groby sighed. The fishing community in Stourhaven was small, Sally knew, and no longer flourishing. Was it credible that they should deliberately harm their reputation,

42

such as it was, by poisoning their meagre harvest? No wonder Groby sighed. 'Oh, well.' He shrugged. 'It will come back to you in time, I hope—but don't worry at it. That never helps anything.' Once more he stood up, preparing to depart. 'And the post mortem'll show if he's been fed poisoned haddock as well as having a knife stuck in him.' He headed back to the door. 'Heaven knows I never had much time for the man, but talk about overkill.'

'Oh.' It had not occurred to her before. 'You know who he is? It wasn't just some—some random lunatic killing a perfect stranger?'

'Terry Spernall was hardly a stranger—and he sure as hell wasn't perfect.' He turned to offer her another wolfish grin. 'And a random lunatic isn't playing fair with the reader, so my wife tells me. Besides, even if it was, they happen in real life about as often as they happen in your books—rather less, if I think about it. Most of us that get bumped off have the bumping done by somebody we know: a member of the family, more likely than not. But Spernall didn't have any family, bar his mother, and he hadn't seen her for a year or more. Been in London, as far as I know.' He shrugged. 'Chances are it was one of his pals from the Smoke that did for him. He's no great loss.'

The eyebrows wagged in surprise at her surprise. 'Terry Spernall was a habitual drunk and a petty villain. As far as I know he wasn't into drugs, but he might as well have been for the trouble he caused. Not one to make headlines with one or two big crimes—he didn't have the brains for that—but I don't know but what a small-time crook niggling away in the background all the time's not worse, in the long run, than your more noticeable type like a bank robber. He certainly upset more people, the way he carried on. Burglary, that's what he was best at when he was sober. Which wasn't often, and at least he didn't drive—brains enough to know he'd kill himself if he did—so it was always the small, valuable stuff that's easy to get rid of and almost impossible to trace. I always suspected he used to take some of it abroad, though I could never prove it when he was still causing trouble in Stourhaven.'

His voice had become harsh, and it was almost as if he were talking to himself. 'Not that it stopped when he left. The opposite, more like . . .' Then he noticed Sally's interest, and bristled at her once more. 'You needn't shed any tears over Terry Spernall. Oh, I'd like to nail whoever it was who killed him because I don't hold with anyone killing anyone else, for whatever reason. But don't ask me to pretend I don't think we're well rid of him. Blokes like him make me sick. When I think of the poor old ladies whose houses they break into and pinch their last little treasures—or the young kids just starting out together, scraping up enough to buy a few bits and bobs for their first home—then in waltzes my lord and helps himself to what they've worked and saved to buy—and the old ladies with their pension books gone along with their memories, the windows smashed and their peace of mind with 'em . . .'

He looked at Sally. 'Got a mobile phone, have you?'

For her peace of mind, of course. 'No, I've never been able to get on with them.'

'Upstairs extension?' he said quickly.

'Yes,' she told him, and saw his shoulders relax.

He nodded at her. 'You didn't see anything; and chummie is miles away, if he's got any sense. He won't come back—he'll know we're on the job by this time. Don't you worry about a thing.' Once more, that grin—meant to reassure, she now had no doubt. 'Well, Miss Jackson, try not to worry—though that's easier said than done, I know. But one burglar the less has got to be good news for the householders around these parts . . .'

And with a few more remarks along the same lines, Superintendent Groby was gone.

CHAPTER FIVE

Sally had been used to smile at eccentric cousins who wedged upturned chairs under their door handles, or set washing-up bowls of cold water under the most easily broken windows to act as a combination booby-trap and burglar alarm.

As she finally made her way up to bed, however, she was not smiling. She found herself in entire sympathy with those cousins. While she had not gone so far as to leave bowls of water on window-sills, she pushed (with an effort that made her wheeze) the heavy blanket-box across her bedroom door once she was inside—if the house caught fire during the night she would have to take her chance—and put the pepper-pot on the bedside table, within easy reach.

She had not expected to sleep; and she did not sleep for more than a few minutes at a time. Her head and eyes ached and she tried to read, but nothing eased the turmoil in her head. Whenever she drifted off, she woke herself again with grim, vivid dreams; and once she was awake she started thinking and could not stop.

It was not just the memory of what had happened that disturbed her. There were too many unanswered questions—and she did not mean simply wanting to know who had killed Terry Spernall . . .

Of course it would greatly help her precarious peace of mind once she knew, not only who had killed Terry, but also—and far more important—that the police had him (or them) in custody. Which was the responsibility of Groby and his minions. But what concerned Sally Jackson now were the personal aspects of the case.

For instance, why had Spernall made his way to her house, of all the houses in that quarter of Stourhaven, to ask for help? Was it because it had been the first he came to? The police seemed to think the attack must have taken place some way out of the town, otherwise somebody, somewhere, would have noticed and reported it long before she had done so.

He had been attacked in one of the nearby woods, perhaps: in which case hers was indeed the first house he would have reached. He would have known there was someone still awake, because of the lights. Yes, there was a reassuring, logical reason for his choosing her house—

But it was not her house. It belonged to the Wellands.

How much did Sally and her globetrotting husband really know about the Wellands? Colleagues from work, she had told Groby. Mrs was a secretary; Mr was another engineer in the welding section. But people with whom you work need not be intimates—and frequently are not. Sally had not disliked the Wellands: on the contrary, they were always friendly when they met at official functions, and the two couples had enjoyed a few drinks together more than once. It had seemed the obvious solution for Sally to house-sit for the first four months of the Wellands' foreign posting after their letting agents had failed to find anyone suitable.

Like Sally and her husband, they had no children: they enjoyed holidays abroad, and this had been the reason they had jumped at the Far East post. They said. But perhaps they had been only too glad of a good excuse to leave the country for a while. Perhaps, once they were safely abroad, they would make a dash for it and never come back . . .

But they had left a lot behind them, for people who had no plans to return: the house, fully furnished; a caravan, which Sally had never seen, except photographed in its discreet woodland setting; a powerful motorboat, which (as far as she knew) was safely dry-docked in some local boatyard for the next twelve months. When the Wellands were not holidaying in foreign parts, or lazing in the sylvan peace of their high class caravan site, they were cruising the coastal waters of the British Isles, with the occasional cross-Channel trip to buy duty-free drinks and exotic foods from the continent.

At this last thought Sally could not help wondering what Mrs Beeton would make of the whole situation. She found the companionship of her shadowy brainchild a comfort in such very uncomfortable circumstances. It had been Mrs Beeton's inspiration that prompted her to hunt out the pepper-pot—in keeping with the Wellands' lifestyle this was a statuesque device of polished wood—and take it upstairs with her to bed. She had no idea how many corns she would have time to grind to hurl in an attacker's face, but failing enough powdered pepper she could always thwack or bop him with it, as Mrs Beeton invariably bopped cornered villains with her gold-plated ladle. And she might be lucky: she might knock him out, and tie him up with a torn pillow case (another of Mrs Beeton's bright ideas), and hand him over to the police in triumph . . .

And this was so delightful—and unlikely—a vision that she found herself, to her amazement, falling asleep.

*   *   *

She slept fitfully for the remainder of the night: yet somehow sleep she did, waking an hour or two later than usual but feeling far less jaded than she might have expected. Mrs Beeton's special soup heap big medicine, especially when served with the golden ladle.

Soup? Her insides lurched. No, she did not fancy soup for breakfast: but tea, and a slice or two of toast—

Perhaps not toast. Or, if yes to toast, then toast with butter only. No jam. Jam was red, and sticky, and—

The telephone rang. She snatched it up.

'Hello?'

'Sally? I am not calling too early, I trust,' came the cordial accents of Mrs Manchester. 'With so much upset last night you will not have slept well, of course, but I have had the police round this morning asking questions . . .' She sounded very proud of this questioning. For a disabled and elderly lady who lived for fifty-two weeks of the year within four brick walls the thought of being a potentially vital witness must have its attractions.

' . . . and I feel so very sorry for you, my dear. Such a terrible shock. As you know, I sleep at the back of the house . . .' Now she sounded regretful. ' . . . so of course I had no idea. I was wondering why Josephine refused to eat her breakfast, and then they told me . . . though no doubt she will change her mind before too long. Cats take such good care of themselves . . .'

She became stern. 'Now I do hope you are taking good care of yourself, my dear, and not being so foolish as to stop eating merely because some unfortunate man expires on your doorstep. What use will it be to him if you

50

starve to death? Have you had anything to eat yet?'

Remembering Superintendent Groby's prophecy about invitations to coffee, there was a smile in Sally's voice as she confessed she had not, as yet, had anything to eat.

'Or drink?' Mrs Manchester might be physically feeble, but there was nothing feeble about her mental processes.

'I was just going to make myself a cup of tea—'

'I have just made one. Come round and share it with me.' It was less an invitation than a command, as Mrs Manchester suddenly seemed to realise. 'It will save you the trouble,' she assured Sally, who almost believed her. 'In the circumstances I have been unable to bake, so bring some biscuits with you, if you have them. And . . .' Now she was as artless as an old lady asking a favour can be. 'Do bring a notebook with you, and a pen. My poor hands, this morning! But you writers are forever complaining how hard it is to think of plots, and I should like to try out a few ideas on you while we have our little snack . . .'

The Wellands had of course briefed their neighbours about their house-sitter before they departed: and Mrs Manchester had been charmed to learn that a genuine published author of detective stories would be coming to live next door. In her almost housebound state, with her stiff, awkward hands, there was not much the old lady could do without discomfort at one level or another, she informed Sally, except read. She had always been a great reader, and now that her pension seemed to stretch less and less far each week . . .

The public library had seen her through many a difficult time, she said, commenting with pride on her good fortune in having her eyesight almost as good now as it had ever been. The van came round each Wednesday and the girls were most obliging, bringing the books in on a tray for her to choose: but with money still in short supply—only now it was the county council—there simply was not the choice there used to be. The history and biography sections had on the whole an acceptable selection, but as for fiction she had often found herself having to read the same book more than once. It was a pity that people like Sally could not manage to write a little faster, though Mrs Manchester quite saw that this was not easy: but had Miss Jackson not said she had started to write detective stories because she enjoyed reading them? Well, then, did Sally think there was any good reason why Regina Manchester should not do the same?

'You never know until you've tried,' Sally told her, and had been invited several times for tea and cakes once the day's word-processor stint was done, when Mrs Manchester chattered happily on about the book she would write one day, if only she had the time, with the house, and the cat, and her fingers less able to hold a pen than they used to be . . .

Mrs Manchester was such a dauntless old lady that her wistful if-only-I-had-the-time did not infuriate Sally as much as this phrase usually does. Any honest author will tell of the jaw-ache suffered when they hear those ominous words and must grit their teeth not to say something rude. But Mrs Manchester's arthritis was painful, Sally could tell. She made light of her handicaps, but they were real. And if her daydreams of authorship made even a few of her difficulties more bearable, who was Sally Jackson to trample those daydreams underfoot?

Idly, she sometimes wondered whether Mrs Manchester might not feel as sorry for Sally— alone in a strange town for four months, her husband away—as Sally felt for her. Had Josephine spent so long in the house when the Wellands lived there? They did not work from home, as Sally did; and they must surely have wished for some time to themselves once their working and commuting were over for the day. Since Sally's time was entirely her own, she had to admit that (when she moderated her numerous demands) Josephine could be most welcome company.

But it was human, not feline, company Sally needed right now, as her next-door neighbour had guessed. And it was not as if the favour would be one-sided. She might never get around to writing her detective story, but there was nothing to stop Mrs Manchester enjoying the idea of living one . . .

'He said something and died?' The old lady's eyes were bright as she nodded at her guest over the teacups. 'How many wonderful books have started that way.' She nodded again, her eyes brighter than ever. 'Films, as well. What about *The Maltese Falcon*?'

'But I thought it was more than halfway through that Captain Jacobi turned up in Sam Spade's office with the falcon,' Sally said, after a moment. 'It's some time since I saw the film, mind you, but I think I remember . . .'

Mrs Manchester chuckled. 'Yes, you do. And he did. I am glad to see your wits have not gone wandering with the shock—as if I ever believed they would, a sensible person like you for all your imagination, my dear. Or at any rate, not for long. Have another of your biscuits, and let us see what else you can remember now you are on the mend—you and Josephine, thank goodness. I was really quite worried about her for a time, but I managed to tempt her appetite with a tasty kipper fillet and—'

Sally's cup dropped into her saucer with a clunk, and a small tidal wave sloshed over the side. She gave a little gasping cry as Mrs Manchester stared at her.

'Not haddock—but I knew it was something to do with fish—he said kipper! He said—he said he ate a kipper! At least . . .' Now the memory was not so clear. Or maybe, now that she spoke it aloud, it sounded too ridiculous. Unless she had misheard, of course. Why would a man who must have guessed he was dying waste his final breath in telling her what he had for supper?

'Write it down!' Mrs Manchester's tone was jubilant. 'But on no account try to force it,' as she saw Sally's frown and shake of the head as remembrance blurred again. 'Try to think about something else, and the rest of it is bound to come, in the end.' She sighed. 'You will, of course, have to tell the superintendent once we have worked it out between ourselves, but there is no reason we—'

She stopped. She had seen Sally's face. 'You did not find him sympathetic, did you? He is an odd character, they tell me, but good at his job.'

'I'm sure he is.' Sally remembered the bristling black stare, and the wolfish grin, and the sudden changes of mood. 'I'm sure he is, but he made me feel . . . he put my back up, a little. He made me uneasy. I don't know why.'

'You are not alone, from what I hear.' Mrs Manchester might well spend most of her time within the confines of her home, but she had an excellent telephonic information network. Very little of what went on in and around Stourhaven escaped her notice when relayed through what she called her Chattery Cattery.

'He achieves results, they tell me, but the man is certainly . . . unusual. Difficult. He has a short fuse—and he is short of staff as well, I understand. Customs and Excise apparently keep asking for help with the smuggling that has started up around here again—oh, dear me, not the occasional cask of brandy,' as Sally gasped at the recollection of Groby's words about trouble not having stopped, quite the opposite, since Terry Spernall left.

'Nobody,' said Mrs Manchester, with a smile, 'pays any heed to that.' Her gaze twinkled in the direction of a set of cut-glass decanters on the sideboard, and Sally had the feeling that in years gone by the contents of those decanters might not have passed inspection by one of HM Customs officers. 'All the local fishermen, you know, will bring in a little extra if the money is right: they always have, they always will. If seafaring folk fare out to sea, they cannot be watched every minute of the day, when there are so many inlets and coves where they may drop off their cargo and have it picked up later by land, leaving the authorities none the wiser. Short of taking their boats away from them, one cannot see how the law could stop them. But—'

This time it was Mrs Manchester's tea that went over the top, but unlike Sally she did not gasp: she squeaked. And it was Sally's turn to stare as the old lady gasped:

'The Wellands' motor-boat!'

CHAPTER SIX

Sally was disconcerted to hear her landlords' next-door neighbour come out with the identical suspicions that had tormented her during those wakeful midnight hours. While she herself hardly knew the Wellands, Mrs Manchester was an old acquaintance. And if an old acquaintance of the Wellands was prepared to accept that Terry Spernall's arrival on Sally's—on their—doorstep might have been deliberate . . .

'But the Wellands are abroad,' Sally said. Perhaps she did not say this as quickly as she could have done. 'And I would have heard if they'd come back. If they'd vanished.' International engineering conglomerates might be complex of structure and ruthlessly impersonal, but they were unlikely to allow employees on whom they had spent generous amounts of relocation money to disappear within a month of arriving at their new location. The uproar caused by such a disappearance would have been apparent even in Sally's part of the world. There would have been e-mails and, time zones permitting, several telephone calls from her husband; and more than several from his superiors. Or more likely from their secretaries. At head office the legal department would consider the possibilities of criminal activity, with Personnel thinking of brainstorms or amnesia; and Sally would have been instructed to keep an eye open for familiar faces with a sinister and shifty—or a lost and vacant—look about them . . .

'But I'm sure they're still abroad,' she said, trying to sound as if she meant it. Which on balance, and (she had to admit) for no logical reason, she thought she did.

With a sigh Mrs Manchester acknowledged her new friend's greater understanding of big business, while clearly reluctant to abandon her theory. The mystery writer in her was coming to the fore as she ventured the courteous objection, 'But, my dear, there is nothing to say the rest of the gang has gone abroad with them, is there?' Her eyes were bright as she began to elaborate. 'Now, let us think. Did they leave the keys of their boat with you? I know you brought your own car with you. But . . .'

'Goodness, I wouldn't have wanted to borrow that great petrol-guzzler of theirs,' Sally assured her. 'Or their boat. Even if they'd offered, which they didn't. I'm no sailor.' She had toyed once or twice since her arrival in Stourhaven with the idea of driving along the coast to one of the ferry ports for a day trip to France. The Channel Tunnel held no attractions whatever for Sally Jackson, but if the sea air might do wonders for the remnants of her bronchitis, the duty-free food and wine would certainly do wonders for her current Mrs Beeton plot. She thought that once she was safely past the Halfway Wall she might indulge herself; but until then it remained just an idea.

'In any case,' she went on, 'as far as I know they've laid up the boat in a local yard until they come back.' Mrs Manchester gave her a thoughtful look. 'It makes sense,' Sally said. 'Even if they trusted me with the responsibility, and there's no reason why they should, I'm only going to be here for a few months. What would happen then? I should think motor-boats must be like cars. If you don't use them regularly, the engine seizes up. Drain the oil and put them in mothballs, and it doesn't. That's why they took one car with them and lent the other to a friend of theirs the other side of Dover, I believe.'

'You believe,' echoed Mrs Manchester, still thoughtful. 'As far as you know. My dear Sally, has it occurred to you that you—we—may be taking a great deal on trust?'

'Well . . . I mean, they trusted me with the house—but—now you mention it . . .'

'The house,' said Mrs Manchester, ticking it off with one arthritic finger against another. 'Rented to you by means, I assume, of a proper legal agreement? Yes,' as Sally nodded confirmation, 'I would expect no less. The Wellands have always seemed a very

59

businesslike young couple.' She ticked a second finger. 'The car, lent to a friend. We believe,' she added, with another look. 'Tell me, my dear Sally. Would such a loan require temporary insurance?'

'I suppose it would—though I'm not sure who has to arrange it,' Sally added. 'It might be the owners of the car, or it might be the person who wants to borrow it. Or both, perhaps.'

'Dear me.' Mrs Manchester's eyes gleamed. 'I know how your profession dislikes coincidence, my dear, but really—*Double Indemnity* and *The Maltese Falcon* in the space of just a few minutes—it must be an omen. How exciting!'

Such enthusiasm was not catching. 'I've had quite enough excitement to last me a lifetime, thank you.'

'We shall see.' Mrs Manchester raised another finger. 'The caravan—on a permanent site, is it not? And, one assumes, rented or let in much the same way as the house?'

'I suppose so,' Sally said. 'It's what they told me. I think. Everything was a bit rushed just before they left, so I don't remember much about it.' She frowned. 'Yes I do, though. Something about duplicate papers in case of emergency—they left a lot of personal stuff in the bureau because they knew I wouldn't be using it. The word processor needs a special table,' she explained to the novelist manqué, who nodded with keen interest as Sally delivered a short lecture on Repetitive Strain Injury.

It was clear Mrs Manchester would bear this risk in mind if ever she started her book. 'Duplicate papers? Photocopies, of course.' She was pleased at her grasp of modern technology. Her eyes shone as she ticked finger number four. 'Duplicate keys too, do you suppose?'

'Oh. Well, if there are, it would be another sensible precaution. But I really have no idea.'

'No,' said Mrs Manchester, pursing her lips as if in disapproval of such ignorance. 'But let us suppose, my dear Sally, that one were to open the desk and find not only the papers inside, but also the keys? Proper keys, rather than duplicates?'

Sally blinked. Was she being encouraged to commit burglary upon the very property signed into her care less than four weeks earlier? 'Even if I could,' she said, 'which I can't because the solicitor has the key, I wouldn't know photocopied documents from the real thing, unless the copies were really cheap and cheerful. Which doesn't sound like the Wellands. And it's no problem to have keys cut, if you can prove title, which I'm sure the Wellands could. Haven't they owned the boat and everything for years?'

Once more Mrs Manchester sighed. 'They have.' Regret for Sally's quenching of her new-born plot was evident in every syllable as she continued: 'I had wondered, you see, whether the finding of papers and keys might not signify a premature return from abroad, already planned without the knowledge of the authorities.'

In fairness, had Sally not wondered something along the same lines? And had tried to dismiss it as too fanciful—

'Or,' continued Mrs Manchester, 'the intention to lend the car, or the boat, to someone for illicit purposes.' Her eyes sparkled, and she leaned eagerly forward. 'Someone who was thwarted last night in his attempt to acquire these items, and—'

'Do stop!' Sally had no wish to hear any more; and not only because as a plot there were far too many holes held together by unnecessarily complicated convolutions. They had been having an almost academic discussion of mystery theory, and now she had been plunged into the remembrance that it was fact, not fiction. 'Do let's talk about something else,' she begged.

The perfect hostess follows the conversational lead of her guest. Mrs Manchester suppressed another sigh, then gave Sally a charmingly sweet smile as she leaned back in her chair. 'Of course, my dear. It was unpardonable of me to forget. There can be no possible excuse, for you are not your usual merry self this morning. Your understandably restless night has left you looking very pale. A brisk walk in the fresh air will,' she said gravely, 'do you the world of good, I feel sure.'

There was something in the way her eyes gleamed . . .

'Perhaps a walk down to the harbour?' Sally enquired.

The gleam became almost mischievous as the watching eyes danced. It was a sad contrast to Mrs Manchester's feeble physical state, but a reminder of the lively young woman she had once been. Three-quarters of a century ago she would never have dropped even this weak pretence at a hint: she would have dragged Sally there bodily, with no discussion. 'Boatyards, my dear, use tar, do they not? Excellent for any weakness of the lungs. Especially after bronchitis.'

Sally smiled into the mischievous depths of those dancing eyes. 'Well,' she conceded, 'it is the first fine morning for ages. And I have to go into town at some point to give a proper statement to the police. But—'

'No buts, my dear. A gentle stroll along the quay to see the sights, followed by—Sally?'

Sally had jumped. She shut her eyes, and knew she was scowling and biting her lower lip as she concentrated. Something was there . . . was coming closer . . .

'Sally! What is it?'

All at once it came. 'Quay!' she cried. 'Not

harbour. He talked about the *quay*—said something about going to sea—and it wasn't haddock or kipper, I'm sure it wasn't, that never did make sense—it was *skipper*. He wasn't trying to tell me what he ate—he said *eight*. Quay number eight, and the skipper would put to sea. I think.' She paused. She thought some more. 'I—I'm sure,' she amended, with Mrs Manchester's bright eyes watching her. 'As far as it goes, that is. There may be more, but for the moment . . .'

'I knew you could do it.' Mrs Manchester's look was a curious mixture of congratulation and apology. 'And you must, of course, tell Superintendent Groby as soon as you can.' The gleam returned, more faintly now. 'No doubt he will warn you against telling anyone else what you have remembered, which is excellent advice.' She paused. 'On the whole.' She paused again. 'Yet I hardly think I count, do you? As a—a security risk, I mean.'

It dawned on Sally that the housebound old lady wanted the fun of hearing that she might be suspected of criminal connections; that her new friend would require proof of her innocence before she would spill any more beans. Mrs Manchester was looking a little frail now; Miss Jackson had no objection to giving her this small pleasure. 'My life,' said Sally, 'is in your hands, Mrs Manchester. Now I've been daft enough to let you know I can identify the rest of the gang . . .'

'But you can't.' The old lady's smile, faint as it now was, faded. 'Can you? Unless, that is, you remember something more . . . because I fear that what you have said makes no sense. I am so sorry. I have lived in Stourhaven for many years, Sally. It is only a small place. Naturally I would expect you to check what I say, my dear, but I have to tell you there are not eight quays in the harbour. And you will find I have told you the truth.'

With puzzled reluctance, Sally subsided. Of course she did not doubt the word of her elderly friend; and yet . . . *Skipper. Quay. Eight. To sea.* She had been so sure.

For a few moments the two sat in a gloomy silence. Sally saw her hostess raise a quick hand to her forehead, and knew it was time to take her leave. As she made to push back her chair, Mrs Manchester frowned. Then she smiled.

'Your—ah—visitor—dear me—last night obviously meant somewhere else,' she announced in triumph, a hint of colour warming her pale cheeks. 'And it should be a simple process of elimination. Along this coast there are many ports and harbours. And quays. It could be Dover, Folkestone, Ramsgate—anywhere bigger than Stourhaven to which he referred. Anywhere with a different . . . layout.' The quiver in her voice was caused by excitement now, rather than exhaustion. 'Think for a moment. You can drive: I can lend you a local atlas. With a little application . . .'

Sally considered the proposal. Yes, it was possible. More than possible: now that Mrs Manchester had set her thinking, it was almost probable.

But was it? 'Or he could,' she said, 'have reverted to childhood. Superintendent Groby said he came from these parts. Maybe the quays were numbered in a different way when he was a child. If we could find a local historian—'

'He was a local man?' The fading eyes snapped into life again as Mrs Manchester sat up. 'But my dear, you made no mention of this before.'

'I didn't remember before.' Sally's tone was apologetic, even though nobody should, she felt, blame her for wanting to leave much of the previous night a merciful blur. 'Spurgeon —Spurling. Spernall. Terry Spernall,' she said with a frown. 'That's who he was.' The dead could not be slandered. 'A villain—petty thief—booze-loving burglar—'

'Who has just lost his mother,' supplied Mrs Manchester promptly. 'That, of course, will be why he was here. In Stourhaven, that is to say, although why he was over this side of town I cannot imagine. Mrs Spernall lived near the harbour.' Once more she leaned forward in her excitement. 'The harbour, Sally! It was in the local paper a few weeks ago. Like me she was disabled, and of an independent mind—which is no bad thing, and why the story particularly caught my eye—but the poor soul died alone at home, and there had to be an inquest because she had not seen a doctor for some time.' She lifted her hand for emphasis. 'And the inquest was adjourned. Now, what do you make of that?'

'Oh!' Mrs Manchester had certainly dropped a bombshell. 'How long ago?'

The old lady closed her eyes and moved her lips as she did mental calculations. 'A month or more,' she offered at last. 'Let us say around the beginning of March. The newspaper reported the inquest and mentioned that the solicitors were looking for her son as the next of kin, putting advertisements in some of the London papers too, because nobody had any idea where he was. Nobody had seen him for a year at least. A bad lot,' she said, unconsciously echoing the words of Superintendent Groby. 'He walked out on his mother—or was thrown, perhaps. One gathers she was a respectable woman. Hardly the sort to want her son involved with gangs of desperadoes burgling houses and stabbing each other all over the place.'

'And the inquest was adjourned.' It was not so unusual, but in the circumstances . . . 'Did the paper say why?'

'I think not. And it is no longer here, I regret to say. As you know, Josephine enjoys exploring the great outdoors, but when the weather is bad she insists on a litter-tray in the kitchen. And you will recall how wet it has been on and off these past few weeks.'

Sally did. The only parts of her rented garden that had laid no claim to minor quagmire status were the raised, well-drained flowerbeds inside their neat brick walls, and the paved paths around them. It was no surprise that Josephine should prefer torn dry newsprint to cold wet mud; but for research purposes it was inconvenient.

'Do you suppose the library might have it on file?'

'Or the newspaper office,' suggested Mrs Manchester, 'if the library has failed to keep it. Having the mobile van call here as I do I am unable to tell you what is kept and what is not. But it should not be so difficult to find out— and it would doubtless be to your advantage if you did so. In person, rather than by telephone.' Once more she found the energy to twinkle, this time with a hint of sympathy. 'Doorstepping, I believe it is called.' She gave Sally no time to cringe at the memory her words invoked. 'Think, my dear.' Sally was trying not to. 'You can surely have no wish to be trapped in the house when the reporters arrive.'

'Oh!' Sally had quite forgotten.

Mrs Manchester had not. 'I imagine they are bound to start pestering once they learn what crime has been committed at the house of an established crime writer. But if you are out of the house all day—well, with any luck they will give up and go elsewhere when the next story breaks.'

With any luck. And Sally was in luck: she was not at home. The press would have no idea where to find her—

'Oh, my goodness!' For the sake of her American tenant in Hertfordshire, she shuddered. 'How awful! It's ridiculous, but somehow I hadn't—' She looked at her watch. 'Mrs Manchester, I've got to go. I have to warn her.'

In normal circumstances her colleague, Sally knew, could be relied on to keep her whereabouts private, if privacy was required. If caught on the hop, however, she might let out more than Sally wanted. She was busy with her research all day, but might not yet have left the house.

If Sally hurried. 'I really must telephone,' she said.

'And I, too, must do a little telephoning,' Mrs Manchester told her, by way of farewell. 'Not all my friends are so retiring as I now have to be.' With cheerful acceptance of her lost mobility she patted the gleaming upright of her walking frame. 'Someone must know something about old Mrs Spernall. What one reads in print is never as much fun as the gossip people will never risk writing down,

69

even though one cannot, of course, libel the dead. While you are taking your little turn at exercise, I will try what a spot of good old-fashioned cattery can do . . .'

She twinkled at Sally one last time as she struggled to slip the latch on the front door. 'We will compare notes later: and we need not inform the superintendent, need we? Unless it is proper evidence, that is. Cast iron—which gossip, naturally, is not. You must tell him all about the eighth skipper putting to sea, of course, but . . .'

'But I don't want him cursing me for interfering,' Sally said. 'Which I have absolutely no intention of doing,' she added firmly. Mrs Manchester must not become carried away, or confuse real life with her favourite fiction. Sally M. Jackson might well have stumbled into a cliché plot—or it (or rather Terry Spernall) had stumbled into Sally—but an even bigger cliché now loomed, one she was anxious to avoid. The brilliant amateur putting one over on the bungling professionals was long departed. Twenty-first century realists had more respect for their skins than to risk them among the modern villains who were nothing like the gentlemen crooks of Mrs Manchester's preferred reading.

Yet it would be churlish to discourage completely one who had been so kind. 'But there's no harm in reading the local paper,' Sally said. 'Or in chatting to your friends . . .'

'We will compare notes later,' said Mrs Manchester, with a nod. 'When I am ready,' she added: it was her first admission of weakness. 'Later,' she repeated; and waved Sally on her way.

CHAPTER SEVEN

Before setting out Sally telephoned the police station, gave her name, and learned that Superintendent Groby was occupied elsewhere. She said she would be along very soon to give her statement, then hung up before too many questions could be asked, sight unseen. Quay Number Eight and the kippery skipper putting to sea would be hard enough to explain face to face. Over the phone they would be impossible.

Sally dialled her home number, but her American colleague must already have left for the day. Nobody answered except her husband's voice on the answering machine, to which she spoke with eloquence, but without going into details. Mrs Manchester's brisk approach to the puzzle of the Corpse on the Doorstep had done wonders for Sally's nerves—and had set her thinking. Callous it might be, but was it not said that in every writer, no matter how tender-hearted, there is a hint of steel? Otherwise known as the nib of a pen.

She would of course have to wait until the case had been safely resolved. Even then she would change all the names, and the general circumstances: but the basics she would not change. She must be honest with herself. There were distinct plot possibilities in what had happened to her the previous night, and—

And suddenly she understood why Superintendent Groby had appeared to view her with such misgiving.

Thinking of Groby made her uneasy. She peered out of the window as if she had just heard him walking up the gravel drive, though all she saw was an ominous blanket of cloud she could have sworn had not been there five minutes before. And had that been a rumble of thunder in the distance?

Perhaps not the ideal morning for a stroll around the harbour; yet heavy weather might not deter the reporters . . .

She took the phone off the hook and muffled its complaining electronic howl under a heap of cushions. She collected her bag, notebook, and keys. She double-locked and treble-checked everything in sight, drove her car from the garage, and headed into Stourhaven to give her official statement.

This proved a relatively painless affair, because Groby continued unavailable. A fresh-faced constable in the first throes of a moustache was on temporary desk duty. He looked up from his careful study of the blotter to greet Sally with a smile she suspected he spent hours practising before the mirror. It was as bright as his regulation buttons, and every bit as proud.

'Good morning, Miss. Madam. Coming on to rain, wouldn't you say? And what can we do for you?'

When Sally told him who she was and why she had come, it took one quick call on the internal telephone to produce a kindly female sergeant, who whisked her off to an interview room, sat her at a table, and offered her a cup of tea. Sally declined the offer with thanks, guessing that no matter what she said the tea would be both strong and sugared when it came. The sergeant said she did not blame Sally in the least, and the coffee was worse. They both giggled. Sally felt a lot better.

'So tell me all about it, Miss Jackson,' invited the sergeant; and Miss Jackson did. The sergeant listened, wrote everything down, and neither bristled nor laughed at Sally for her fancies. The sergeant had never heard of a Quay Eight: but who was to say the dead man had been speaking of Stourhaven? It was more than likely he had meant somewhere else. Terry Spernall had relatives abroad, and often used to visit them when he still lived at home.

'Strong family ties,' said the sergeant, with a knowing look Sally was at liberty to interpret as she chose. With a nod she implied that she knew something of Superintendent Groby's smuggling problem. The sergeant winked.

'Travel broadens the mind, they say,' she said cheerfully, going on to remark that, talking of minds, she would recommend a change of scene to take Miss Jackson's mind off things. And promised she would be one of the first to know if—hastily, she corrected herself—when whoever had killed Terry Spernall was caught.

That hasty correction was enough to remind Sally M. Jackson that this was not one of her books: this was real life, and she was in the middle of it.

She decided she preferred the printed page.

After leaving the police station she headed for the library to ask for the past six weeks of the local paper. It did not take long to check the file. The inquest report on Mrs Spernall was as uninformative as she had feared it might be; she filled only half a page of her spiral notebook with details including the lady's full name (Edith Dagmar Elisabeth), her age, and her address, which Sally checked in the county street-by-street atlas in the reference section. Mrs Manchester had been right: Mrs Spernall had lived, and died, down by the harbour.

'Are there any detailed maps of Stourhaven harbour?' she asked, hoping she did not sound foolish and wondering too late if charts would have been the more correct form.

'Maps of the harbour?' Sally had gone from one extreme of enquiry (the trainee constable) to the other in the form of the elderly head librarian, a stranger to Sally as Sally was to her. She was a stern, faded little lady with a voice trained by years of obeying Silence notices to a hush that was at the same time both efficient and clear-toned.

'Maps of the harbour?' The head librarian blinked over the top of her gold-rimmed spectacles as she moved out from the Enquiry desk. Sally observed her below-the-knee tweed skirt and her sensible shoes. She had drawn the line at lisle stockings, but her knitted cardigan was perfect for the part. Sally wondered about the head librarian . . .

'We have here on file,' said Miss Gold Rims, leading Sally to a large, flat cabinet, 'the Ordnance Survey sheets for the district in three different sizes. One inch, six inches and twenty-five inches to the mile.' From the way she primmed her lips it seemed she had as little sympathy for the metric system as had Sally. 'That would give you a certain amount of detail. What exactly was it you were looking for? I might be able to find you something more suitable if . . .'

'The Ordnance Survey sounds fine, thank you, unless—well, what I really want to know is how many quays there are in Stourhaven harbour. And how they're—um, identified.'

Another gold-rimmed blink, accompanied

75

by an upward rush of pale moth eyebrows. 'How many quays?' echoed the head librarian. 'Let me see. There's the East Mole, and the West Mole, and the Breakwater in the middle. I suppose you could call them quays, though I've never heard anyone do so. Jetties, sometimes, but never quays.'

'Just the three.' Mental arithmetic had already told Sally that double would be too few; three times would be too many. Eight. Quay eight . . .

'Berths, on the other hand—' Gold Rims was determined to be helpful. 'There must be, oh, twenty or twenty-five berths along each mole, and more on the Breakwater. They're identified by numbers, as far as I recall.' She shook her head in disapproval of this non-literal scheme. 'I'm afraid we have no map or plan in our library that would show them individually, if that's what you want.' She glanced over her shoulder at the telephone on the Enquiry desk. 'The harbour master is sure to have more detailed information, of course. Would you like me to ask him?'

'Er—oh.' Sally felt awkward at the suggestion, without knowing why. 'That's all right, thank you. It wasn't very important. Maybe I'll take a stroll down there this afternoon and have a look for myself, if the rain keeps off.'

The pale eyebrows arched again. 'If the rain keeps off? In England? In April?' The head librarian's chuckle was full and hearty. 'This close to the Grand National?'

Sally had been right in hesitating to prejudge the book by its conservative library cover. In her cliché costume—under the knitted cardigan she wore a blouse with a pussy-cat bow—Miss Gold Rims might have seemed a most unlikely person to be interested in the greatest steeplechase in the world; but the old saying about appearances held good, as it did for Sally too. She knew only two things about the horse (and one of them was rather coarse) but even she had risked an occasional flutter on the National over the years, though her main sporting interests lay elsewhere.

'Close to the Boat Race, too,' she replied, and knew she had not underestimated her woman. The gold rims gleamed as Miss Jackson went on, 'Not that a drop of rain is going to worry them, unless they can't bail fast enough.'

Another hearty chuckle from Miss Gold Rims; it might be more accurate to say she giggled. 'Oh, yes. Remember when Oxford sank that time?'

'And when Cambridge steered into another boat and sank before the start?'

'And . . .'

Before she knew it Sally was swapping happy reminiscences of My Favourite Boat Race (she could not compete on Grand National terms) with someone who confessed that if she was unable to wangle the relevant Saturdays off each spring, she would sneak a portable radio into work and retreat to the privacy of the cubby-hole called the Old Catalogue Room, the five-by-three cards now superseded by a computer system but maintained by herself less from nostalgia than from a distrust of too much reliance on computer technology. Sally's heart warmed to the kindred spirit of Miss Gold Rims, who was suddenly another person. She lost twenty years in as many seconds; ignored the chirp of the Enquiry telephone as she talked; and when Sally at last managed to bring the conversation to an end, chuckled and winked as if they shared some secret vice her colleagues could never understand. She bet Sally five pounds that it would be a Cambridge win this year, while Sally held out, as she always did, for the Dark Blues. Miss Jackson left the library vowing to return the Monday after the race to collect her winnings, and Gold Rims chuckled again as she waved her on her way.

The head librarian's prediction had been correct: it was raining, and heavily, as Sally went through the swing doors into the street. Mentally, she shrugged. Sleuthing in fine weather might be one thing. Asking what they would doubtless regard as absurd questions of complete strangers when it was cold and grey and miserable did not promise to yield particularly good results. She would treat herself to a few tasty somethings from the local delicatessen, pick up a magazine or two from the newsagents, and go home—no—go back to the Wellands' house—

'Back to work,' she told herself firmly. 'After the deli.' She must not indulge in speculation about her landlords. She must be sensible. She must leave everything to the police . . .

Once at the house she unpacked her shopping and loaded the perishables into the fridge. The kipper fillets—for Josephine, if it ever stopped raining—she re-wrapped in a double layer of cooking foil and snapped into a supposedly smell-proof plastic box with an airtight lid. She checked the telephone: still off the hook, its indignant howl still muffled. She made a cup of tea, and resolved to celebrate her peaceful solitude with a few hours' work.

The rain had not stopped as towards the end of the day she tried ringing Mrs Manchester to tell her what little she had learned. She tried several times, but the line was always engaged. The old lady was probably still busy with her cattery chattery—or else was trying to ring Sally, who each time she got the engaged tone broke the connection and did not replace the handset on the cradle. She was happy to talk with Mrs Manchester, but not yet with anyone else. After the events of the past twenty-four hours she needed to let her brain cool down. In the end, once she felt calm enough, she could face the thought of talking to people: but she was still far from calm, despite several cups of tea as she worked, and two large glasses of wine with supper.

When she went up to bed she tried to read, found her eyes blurring, polished her glasses with a freshly-laundered cotton handkerchief, found it made no difference, switched off the light and then lay tossing in a resolutely unbarricaded room listening to the rain, not sleeping a wink, wondering what she was trying to prove. And to whom. And why. At last she gave up, hopped out of bed, glared at the blanket-box and compromised on a chair, telling herself even as she wedged it under the doorhandle that she was being foolish.

She checked the bedside phone. She had replaced the downstairs handset so that the line was no longer blocked for outgoing calls, then repeated her muffling act in the bedroom with a blanket rather than cushions. The dialling tone buzzed reassurance in her ear. Yes, if the desperadoes broke in she could ring for help.

Unless they cut the line.

She would not think about that.

She would think instead that she must try to overcome her dislike of mobile phones. She wondered which of her friends could give advice on the best model. Her change from an electric typewriter to a word processor some years ago had been less intimidating than might have been expected—but Sally had had moral and technical support at home when she took that particular plunge. Now, with her husband away—

Like the Wellands—

'No!' She switched on the light, and struggled to read one of her magazines. Her sight was still blurred, her eyes still weary; her brain was not. She felt hot and cold by turns as she lay down again. Her feet were restless, the bottom sheet grew rumpled, the duvet developed a will of its own and was sometimes too heavy, sometimes too thin. Had she in an absent-minded moment—and goodness knew she had every excuse to be absent-minded—had she somehow altered the thermostat on the radiator?

For the second time she hopped out of bed, padding across in her bare feet to the window, where she lifted a corner of the curtain and peered out into what was no longer a rainy night. The sky was clear; the light from stars and moon and street lamps glistened on roofs and pavements and puddles. She blinked and rubbed her eyes at the fuzzy, fairy-tale glow of reality that replaced the bleak nightmare scene she had feared. A blacker-than-shadow shadow, Josephine on the prowl, slipped from one pool of pavement light to the next; was gone.

If Josephine, upset as she had been the night before, now showed no fear as she approached the house, it was not for Sally

Jackson inside, with a telephone—and a chair wedged under the door—to ignore the little cat's example. Without checking the thermostat, Sally went back to bed.

Once more she closed her eyes, curling herself into a comfortable shape and pulling the duvet over her ears. She was tired. She would sleep.

Terry Spernall crawled from pool to pool of pale pavement light, one hand ever groping, groping ahead as if he were already blind— blind with the nearness of death. Sally woke with a start as his hand gripped her ankle; as the nails dug into her flesh. A cadaveric spasm—in someone who wasn't yet dead—

Not for worlds could she reach out to switch on the bedside lamp. She knew that before her hand found its target it would be clasped by another, icy cold, clammy with blood.

A groping, spectral hand with piercing nails—

Then she heard the scratching.

CHAPTER EIGHT

It was the cheerful jangle of the milk float that persuaded her it might be safe to emerge from the quivering cocoon into which she had retreated at some point during that tense and awful night. When she had managed to fall asleep, she had no idea. How much sleep she had had, she could not say. She felt more than tired; she was exhausted.

This could not go on. She had work to do, creative work for which her subconscious had to be kept sternly in check, not allowed to erupt into overdrive and hysteria. Imagination could—and had—run riot in the dark, in that house. She must not allow herself to become its victim. She must get right away for a while: she would phone round, find a suitable hotel, and tell nobody except the police where she was going. Mrs Manchester was a spirited old lady, but frail. Sally did not want her bullied by reporters—

Or by anyone else.

'I won't think about that,' Sally announced to her unruly subconscious. 'I'll have a cup of tea. Fresh milk: a fresh start.'

Duly washed and dressed she went to the door to fetch the bottle from the front step.

The bottle smashed in pieces to the ground.

White blood trickled—

No. Milk. She had dropped the bottle.

She had seen fresh scratches in the bottom corner of the door—

She leaped back inside, slammed the door, and breathed deeply in and out, in and out while she made her unsteady way to the kitchen—fetched a cloth, a bucket, a bowl, a mop—forced herself back down the hall to open the door. She dropped the cloth to soak

83

up the milk, shook slivers of glass into the bucket, soaked and shook, soaked and shook. She poured hot water from the bowl, and mopped. She closed the door on a damp, steaming step.

She did not permit herself even one glance at what common sense told her had no reason to be scratches in the bottom corner of the front door.

At the kitchen sink she washed the mop, rinsed the bowl, strained the bucket through a sieve. She wrapped the glass in newspaper, wound sticky tape around the bundle in case it unwrapped itself and made holes in the black plastic liner of the dustbin: it would never do for Josephine to cut her prowling paws through Sally's carelessness . . .

Dear Josephine. Was she still prowling, or had she gone home? Prowling, probably. The daughter of a pure-bred white Persian who had succumbed to the whiskery wiles of the midnight tom from three houses down, Josephine had inherited her parents' wanderlust.

'Josephine. Of course!'

The scratches.

Sally sighed with relief. Poor damp, chilly little cat: realising her mistress would find it difficult to hobble through the house at midnight to let her back into the warm, she had come instead, once the rain had stopped, to Sally. Josephine, wise creature, excellent example, had no foolish qualms about using the door where a man had died. Sally's bedroom was directly above that door. Josephine had known she would be heard: and Sally had heard her.

And ignored her. Poor damp, chilly little cat.

Heading with her newspaper bundle for the outside bin Sally glanced through the kitchen window into the bright warmth of the back garden. Josephine. In a corner where two brick flowerbeds met, curled in a black, fluffy, prick-eared mound on the sun-warmed paving stones, Mrs Manchester's cat lay sheltered from the whispering April breeze, fast asleep.

Sally pulled the back door bolt, and Josephine's ears twitched. Sally unlocked the door, and the little cat's head went up.

Her head went up and she uncurled, in one movement so swift she was nothing but a black furry blur spinning in mid air to land four-square on her sturdy paws.

Swift: not swift enough. Sally's mouth opened in horror as her mind caught up with what she had just seen. Two pricked ears, two bright eyes, one fluffy body . . .

But no plumy tail.

'Joseph—!'

Sally never finished. She could not.

The little cat was barking too loudly for her to hear herself think.

Barking?

Josephine?

Sally did not move, which instinct told her was the best thing to do as Jo— as the little black tailless dog rushed across the lawn, still firing a volley of barks as she drew closer.

Or was it 'he'? If s/he ever stayed still for more than a few seconds Sally might find out. Her instinct began to suggest 'he': those barks were surprisingly deep, from such a small frame. It was hard to tell, with so much rushing and dancing as the dog reached the back doorstep and began leaping round her ankles. She judged him (or her) to be rather larger than Josephine, who was a well-fed yet dainty specimen inside her part-Persian fur. Twelve pounds or a little more, Sally guessed. About the same size, fluffy and black and in her favourite corner: no wonder she had made what now was so obviously a mistake.

Sally went on not moving and the little dog went on dancing about her feet, though by now he had stopped barking in favour of sniffing. As his shiny black nose quested, his breath came in snuffles and snorts. Around his neck the fur stood out in a proud yet rather bedraggled ruff; his rounded tailless rump, clad in what reminded Sally of black feathery culottes, began to waggle. He snorted some more, waggled his bottom harder, lifted his head and glared at Sally from bright, strangely blue-tinged eyes.

He barked: one quick, deep command,

followed at once by a lowering of his head and a snap of his jaws round the hem of Sally's jeans. He tugged. He let go, looked up, and barked again. He stood absolutely still, watching her. In the soft spring breeze his black ruff rippled in time with the feathers at his back.

'Hello,' Sally said. Slowly, she bent her knees until she could rest comfortably on her heels. The little dog continued to watch as, still slowly, she held out her hand for him to sniff.

Leaning forwards and up, throwing most of his weight on his front feet, he sniffed. He sniffed again, his nose damp and cold against her skin. His back legs splayed out behind him at what seemed an odd angle: viewed sideways, he would have looked like a lopsided trapezium, broad-shouldered and slim-hipped, with his neck muffled into invisibility by the fur of the ruff that framed his head.

'Friends?' enquired Sally as he gave one final sniff and then eased his back legs forwards in a quaint shuffling motion, balanced himself, and gave her hand a quick lick. She tickled him under his chin. He did not flinch. She rubbed his powerful chest, and he blinked. As she stood up, he neither barked at her nor jumped away. Friends.

'Like to come indoors?' The little dog wore no collar: though the thickness and length of his ruff would have concealed all but the widest band, Sally's tactful inspection had shown there was no identification there. 'Do you fancy a snack? A biscuit?'

His ears pricked and swivelled, flattening against his domed skull and standing up again. He began to breathe in grunting gasps.

'Biscuit?' Sally moved back to the door, with the dog close behind. Once they were both safely over the threshold she pushed the door shut. The catch caught with a sharp click, and the dog's ears flicked as his head immediately searched for the source of the sound.

Once he recognised it he appeared to have no objection to being held captive. His bright eyes scanned the kitchen in one quick look and then he began to explore, his nails clattering cheerfully on the tiles as he sniffed the base of every cupboard door and found his way to the refrigerator.

His way. Yes, now that Sally had seen him closer he was definitely male. Mostly male. She knew more of cats than dogs, but the basics were not so different; it was clear he had been neutered. She felt sure this could not have been because of his temperament, as he appeared to be a delightful, merry little dog; she guessed it was a breeding problem. She watched him pattering on his kitchen progress and observed that he limped with his left hind leg, not putting it properly to the ground, walking only on his toes.

'Hip dysplasia,' said Sally, whose sister-in-law walked Guide Dog puppies and had lent her several books. 'Maybe,' she added as the little dog whisked round and dashed over to her. Reminded by Sally's voice of her presence, he had been reminded of her promise. She went to the tin. Its opening rattle seemed to interest him.

'Josephine enjoys chocolate digestives,' she told him. 'But I read a mystery where someone tried to kill a dog by feeding him human chocolate, so I'm giving you a Garibaldi, if that's all right. Flour and raisins and a sprinkle of sugar shouldn't do you too much harm.'

She offered the biscuit without thinking, but he did not snatch. He tilted his head, mouthed at her hand, and folded his lips over what his teeth had seized before tugging for release, and retreating a few inches to eat his prize. It was crunched and gone in an instant. Sally's visitor then polished the floor with vigour and a long pink tongue, and looked up at her for more.

He was panting. She was cross with herself. 'You're thirsty?' Not milk, for dogs: she remembered that, too. Besides, with having dropped the new bottle she had barely enough for her morning cup, which held an imperial pint and needed more than a splash of milk.

She opened a cupboard to find a bowl, and at once an inquisitive black head thrust its way in beside her. Again without thinking she pushed the little dog out of the way. He skittered, but did not snap. No. Not a problem

89

with temperament.

A bite to eat, a drink of fresh water: what else would a stray dog need? She reached down to stroke his head.

With a piercing yelp he darted away. Many dogs dislike being approached from above: but Sally had stroked him from the flank. She studied him as carefully as he now watched her, in case she should hurt him again.

Partly hidden by the lavish ruff, one side of his head was swollen. Bruised, but with the skin undamaged. He had been hit: perhaps by a car, perhaps by the person who had taken off his collar and abandoned him. If that was what had happened.

'You might have slipped out through someone's door,' Sally said. 'You're so quick. And people can be so careless.' She shivered. 'And some can be so cruel.'

She resumed her gentle under-the-chin tickling, and they were starting to relax together when the doorbell suddenly rang. The little dog performed another roundabout whisk, flung up his head, and hurtled out of the kitchen down the hall towards the source of the ringing, barking even more loudly than he had barked when Sally first disturbed him in the garden. He skidded to a halt under the letterbox and began to bounce up and down towards the handle. No doubt in his mind where the enemy would force an entrance.

He was so lively and quick that Sally was

unable to get close to peer through the frosted glass skylight without tripping over him. Enemy or friend on her front step, she would not find out until she opened the door. The thought did not disturb her. Anyone hearing the racket from behind that door would think she had a posse of trained Alsatians to protect her. She would take the risk.

She swooped on her still-bouncing protector, tucked him as well as she could under one arm, and started to open the door. It was not easy. Four sturdy legs kicked wildly in all directions as the little dog tried to leap from her arms to the floor and (she supposed) through the widening gap to savage the ankles of whoever had dared to invade her—his— their territory.

So close to her face, his barks were deafening. She clamped her free hand over the dog's muzzle as soon as she could. The barks subsided to a furious strangled yodel, deep in the little dog's throat.

'Er—good morning. Sally Jackson?' The stranger outside had taken a wary few steps backwards as that ferocious little black face came into view.

Stranger? In himself he was a stranger, but Sally had a good idea *what* he was: perhaps the pungent aroma of tobacco betrayed him. However she knew, she knew him for a reporter. Maybe only from the local paper, tipped off by someone at the police station that there had been an interesting entry in the occurrence book: but local stories reached the national press, as any reader knew.

The dog wriggled and kicked and yodelled in Sally's arms. He might weigh little more than a cat and resemble nothing so much as a cut-price Pomeranian, but he made it very plain that he would not hesitate to stand up to this intruder if only Sally would put him back on the ground.

This dauntless example encouraged her. She crossed mental fingers against the lie and answered, 'No,' with as much conviction as she could, giving the little dog a grateful squeeze as she spoke.

'Oh?'

It was better than 'Are you sure?', which she had heard some people say. As if one would not be.

'Are you sure?' The yodels, and that ferocious glare, must have made him get his lines in the wrong order.

'Yes!' Sally had to shout above the noise, and unusually for an author sent up a silent prayer of thanks that he had obviously never read her books. The jacket photograph would have betrayed her at once.

'But I was told she was staying here!'

'Well, so she was!' Sally was no actress, and no good at impromptu prevarication, but with luck he would blame the wriggling bundle in her arms for any agitation she might be showing. 'She—she went away this morning!' Inspiration had struck. 'And asked me to come and look after her dog!'

'Has she gone abroad, then?'

It was a logical question, as they were on the Channel coast. 'She didn't tell me! She said she'd phone when she found somewhere she liked! She could be anywhere!'

'When will she be back?'

Prevarication was becoming an effort. Sally allowed her hand to slip from the little dog's muzzle. His mouth opened wide as he roared, showing sharp white teeth and a ravening red tongue. The reporter took another step back. It must be that the shouted exchange had upset Sally's canine armful, for he showed no signs of calming down.

For which Sally thanked goodness.

'I'd better take him in! Excuse me! Goodbye!' And she managed to slip inside and slam the door before it could occur to the reporter that she could easily have shut the dog away in another room while she was interviewed.

Then she saw the way the dog, still barking, scrabbled with his forepaws at the doormat, trying to dig his way out to see off the intruder. Even had Sally wished to talk, it would have been no easy job to conduct an interview in peace and quiet.

'You,' she told the little dog firmly, 'are a very good boy. Good, and brave, and useful.

Come and have another biscuit—you deserve a little something for your trouble.'

And he bounced down the hall beside her as she made her way happily back to the kitchen.

CHAPTER NINE

He was at the biscuit tin before her, his ears flicking to and fro, his nose wuffling. Sally gave him another Garibaldi and saw it disappear as fast as the other had done.

'You deserve something better after that performance,' she told him. The ears flicked again, and the little head tilted to one side as if serious consideration was being given to what she had said. Perhaps it was. If cats could read human thoughts, why not dogs?

Cats. Josephine. What she didn't know would not hurt her. 'How about a nice kipper?'

The ears flicked, the bright eyes gleamed, the bouncing began again. The little dog barked, in quite a different way from the way he had barked before.

'Kipper?'

Flick, bark, bounce.

'Is that your name? Kipper? Hello, Kipper.' Sally bent to stroke him, avoiding his poor swollen head, and he licked her hand. 'Kipper,' she said, and he licked her again.

'Biscuit?'

Flick, bounce. No bark. She was right. Kipper he was.

'It seems almost cannibal,' she remarked as she took the plastic box from the refrigerator and prised off the lid. 'But I promised; and you do look hungry. Hang on while I warm this for you. If cats shouldn't eat straight from the fridge I don't suppose dogs should, either.'

Kipper devoured his namesake snack with every evidence of relish. He left the bowl empty and shining, and Sally's ankles feeling sore. He had not cared for the wait while she removed all the kipper bones and boiled the kettle, and kept swiping sideways at her with his head to nudge her into swifter action.

Only one side. That swelling, bruise, whatever it was still caused him some discomfort. His owners really ought to let him be seen by a vet.

His owners. No collar. Out all night—

'Last night!' And realisation came. It must have been Kipper, not Josephine, whose black shape had crossed Sally's line of out-of-focus vision in the wakeful midnight hours.

He was a stray.

Was he?

He was an excellent watchdog.

If Sally had lost a dog like this she would have reported him lost as soon as she noticed he had gone—which, with a dog like Kipper, would be immediately. Which would mean yesterday. Twelve hours ago, at least: maybe twenty-four.

She went to the telephone, surprised at how loudly her heart thumped as she sat down to dial, and Kipper nuzzled close to her feet. Her free hand drifted down to rumple the ruff around his neck.

'Is that the police? Could I speak to whoever keeps the lost dogs register?'

A kindly baritone. 'Duty Sergeant here.' Young Moustaches was not in evidence today. 'You've lost a dog?'

'No, I've found one. A little black dog, rather fluffy, a bit bigger than a cat, without a tail.'

The baritone was not so kindly now. 'You're saying some devil's cut his tail off?'

'Oh, sorry—no, he's been properly docked. I think his head's been hurt, though. One side seems very swollen, but his fur's too thick to be sure. I wondered if perhaps he'd been thrown out of a car—been dumped, you know.'

'Oh yes, I know.' The duty sergeant's normal baritone was a basso profundo growl as he spoke in the tones of an animal-lover. 'No tail,' he said again, more easily now.

'And no collar, either—but I think his name might be Kipper.' A warm wet lick on Sally's free, stroking hand. 'Has—' she found her voice catching—'has anyone rung in to say they've lost him?'

'Haven't had a lost dog reported in weeks, my dear.'

96

'Oh!'

The sergeant chuckled. 'Someone sounds happy. Taken a shine to him, have you?'

'Yes I have, rather.' And he to her, Sally thought, as another lick was followed by a shuffle of Kipper's whole body and he slumped against her ankles to let her scratch him behind his unharmed ear.

'It's Saturday,' said the sergeant thoughtfully. 'Look, you couldn't hang on to him until Monday, could you? Makes the paperwork easier if we can send him straight over to the council pound instead of keeping him here. We haven't the proper facilities for dogs at the station, you see, and with Saturday night always being a bit lively . . .'

'Oh.' The council pound: Sally's imagination showed her a lonely wire cage, a cold, concrete floor and a bowl of scraps. For a happy little dog like Kipper? 'Well, yes of course I'd be glad to keep him.' She gulped. 'To keep him for good, if nobody . . . He's so friendly—and a wonderful burglar alarm,' she added, sure this would appeal. 'How do I go about staking my claim, or whatever you have to do?'

'You give me your name and address, and the date you say you found him, and if nobody asks after him within the week you pay fifty pounds to the council, and he's yours.'

Fifty pounds: around four pounds sterling for each pound avoirdupois. 'And worth every penny,' Sally said firmly. 'I'd love to keep him, if I can.'

The sergeant chuckled richly. 'Let's hope you can, then. Sounds to me as if Kipper's fallen on his feet with you, my dear. So what's your name?'

'Sally Jackson.'

'Oh.' A pause. 'Ah.'

'Yes,' she said, answering the unspoken question. 'The one who's been seeing such a lot of your colleagues in the past couple of days.'

Another pause. 'Well, my dear, I'd say if anyone needs a dog for company right now, it's you. Kipper, eh? When did you find him?'

'I first saw him,' she replied warily, 'yesterday. Friday.' Very late on Friday, but so what? This prevarication was becoming a habit.

'Only six days to go, then,' said the sergeant cheerily. 'I somehow don't think you'll have too much bother keeping him. Most folk in these parts, they take care of their dogs. Friday. Well, I'm sure we'd have heard by now if he'd slipped his collar and got out of the house through a door left open.' He coughed. 'Dumping's far more likely, poor little beggar, with a bump on his head and all. You'll be taking him to a vet?'

'Yes, my next door neighbour has a cat, so I'm going to ask her to recommend someone.'

'Ah,' said the sergeant slowly. 'Yes. Well, there's cat vets, Miss Jackson, and there's dog vets. Fair to all sorts of animal, of course, but easier with one than t'other. You could do far worse than take this Kipper of yours to young Harry Christopher, down by the harbour. He's got a surgery Saturday evenings, and he don't charge too much.' His tone became confidential. 'Go there myself with mine, and he's done wonders with her—waterworks, poor old girl. She's twelve and it was a real problem, but now you'd swear she was a youngster again. Take her every Sunday right round the golf-course, I do, and that's four miles if it's an inch.' The metric system, Sally thought with approval, had a long way to go to become established in Stourhaven. 'He's a fine vet, young Harry. You tell him Sergeant Biggin sent you, and he'll see you both right.'

'Thank you very much, Sergeant Biggin. Thank you!' And Kipper lifted his head and blinked at Sally, and flicked his ears, and almost seemed to purr.

She looked up the number, phoned the vet, and heard from his answering machine that the surgery opened at six. She and Kipper had a few hours still in which to become better acquainted. She took him back out to the kitchen for more biscuit; when he had eaten it, and had another drink, he went to the door and barked.

'Hmm,' said Sally. A dog who could find his way in the dark into a garden could certainly find his way out again in daylight. She told him to wait, and went off in search of a thin leather belt. Rather than wait he trotted after her, checking every inch of the house as he passed along the hall and up the stairs. In her bedroom he made to cock his leg against the chair, then caught her eye, and looked abashed. The phrase 'marking his territory' came to Sally's mind, and she hoped—wondered—about omens.

Having returned to the kitchen and found a ball of string she fashioned a rough collar from the belt, attached the string, and took Kipper outside into the sunshine she had been too busy before to notice. A perfect gentleman, the little dog moved away from the house before cocking his leg for the official performance, and Sally saw that as he walked the limp did not seem to bother him even though his left hind toes only brushed the ground, and if she walked too fast he almost hopped to keep up with her.

Together they explored the garden, where beside a shrub Sally noticed a small deposit that did not appear to be the responsibility of Josephine, who always buried them. Back indoors for a plastic freezer-bag; scoop, twist, tie a knot, into the bin. If Sally was destined to become a dog owner she would start the way she planned to go on.

Josephine's face appeared fleetingly under the hedge, but vanished before Kipper saw her. If he stayed, she might never visit Sally again. Miss Jackson was surprised at how little this distressed her. She knew she could always pop next door to see her . . .

But not today. Mrs Manchester had seemed weary indeed by the end of yesterday's chat, and there had been her promise to meet again 'later'. She had told Sally at their first meeting that when things were not going too well with her it took several days before she felt human again: she might struggle to the door for Josephine's sake, but not for anyone else. Sally had mentioned a cat flap, but when she learned how Badroulbadour, Josephine's mother, had behaved with Black Tom from down the road it did not surprise her that Mrs Manchester had instructed her odd-job man to block off the flap he had fitted only a fortnight or so earlier.

'I wouldn't have hanky-panky problems with you,' Sally said to Kipper as he anointed a clump of grass. 'I wonder if you could use a cat flap? Not that the Wellands would be too pleased if I had holes cut in their kitchen door, of course. But once I'm home again—'

No. She was tempting fate; getting much too far ahead of herself. She must remember there were another six days to go before Kipper became hers. If he did. Irrationally, she was glad she had continued to leave the telephone off the hook. She did not want the police station to ring to tell her Kipper's owners had turned up.

If anyone had failed to reach her by phone,

they had made no personal appearance at the house by the time Sally and Kipper set out for the surgery of Harry Christopher, veterinary surgeon. They went on foot. It seemed another way of furthering their acquaintance; moreover, the lively little dog might prove a distraction to a driver still unsettled by recent events.

They had not walked far before Sally wondered if she had made a mistake. For his size Kipper was a powerful animal, with a massive chest and well-muscled shoulders under that thick, glossy coat. As he pattered and snuffled and pulled his way down the road Sally began to worry that her makeshift string-and-belt contrivance might not hold until they reached the harbour. Harry Christopher could perhaps lend her a proper collar and lead until she could confidently buy her own and take Kipper to training class . . .

But that was in the future: this was now. Should she go back and fetch the car, after all? But Kipper's behaviour in a moving vehicle was still an unknown quantity, and might be dangerous. One unexpected bounce . . .

She had ruled out any idea of asking Mrs Manchester for help, and not only because of her frailty. Sally was sure Josephine would strongly disapprove if her handsome wicker travel basket came back smelling of unknown canine; and she suspected Kipper would disapprove just as strongly of being put inside a basket smelling of cat. They would chance it and walk on, and if necessary take a taxi home. Kipper had happily cuddled close to Sally's feet when she was on the phone; he could cuddle and be stroked just as well in a car.

They were not the first to arrive at the surgery, which Sally found without difficulty. Apart from one or two pubs on the waterfront it was the only commercial building with lights on and cars (four) parked outside. She pushed open the door, and dragged Kipper—who was hanging back to savour the rich fishy, salty, tarry-rope bouquet of Stourhaven harbour— up the steps and inside.

Three wooden benches lined three poster-decked walls of the room; the fourth wall sported floor-to-ceiling shelves packed with merchandise. There was a desk in front of the shelves, to one side of a door Sally guessed led through to the surgery proper. In the middle of each bench sat a solitary human being: one sad-eyed male, two females with poker faces. All three stared at Sally and Kipper as they entered, then returned their attention without speaking to the boxes and baskets on their laps. No other dogs. Good. Kipper seemed unsettled enough by the long-established smell of disinfectant and animal agitation.

The girl behind the desk looked up from her computer. 'Do you want to see the vet? He's running a bit late this evening, but if it's a repeat prescription I can handle it. Or is it an emergency?'

They had walked all the way. 'No, I don't think so.'

'Oh well, take a seat.' She fiddled with her mouse and looked at the screen. 'Have you been before?'

'No,' said Sally. 'And I'm not sure—'

'Oh, don't worry,' said the girl. 'Mr Christopher likes to give people time to make up their minds before he takes them on the books properly.' Sally could see the advantages from Mr Christopher's side, as well as that of the people. 'If you get on okay you can give me your details when you come out,' the girl went on. 'Otherwise, you just pay.' She jerked her head towards the door beside her desk. 'It's turns to go in. You'll be fourth, after everyone else.'

Miss Jackson wondered which of the middle-benchers would be first to crack, and shift to one side so that she could take her seat as instructed. It was an intriguing puzzle: to which she never had the answer. As six reluctant feet were starting a half-hearted shuffle the inner door opened, and a red-faced man with a squeaking cardboard box came out. At once the thinner of the two poker females jumped up to stake the claim nobody else was about to dispute.

The cardboard squeak rocked and scrabbled as the man put it on the desk and prepared to settle his bill. Kipper's nose twitched. The box rocked some more. Sally feared it might fall off the desk and allow the occupant to escape, but the receptionist moved faster than she would have expected and grabbed with both hands to stop the rocking.

'You really should be more careful,' she scolded the red-faced man, whose face grew even redder as he tried to become invisible. 'You know what happened last time.'

Blushing hotly he confessed his fault, paid the money, seized the box and was gone. Sally wondered what had happened on the occasion of his last visit. Killer Hamster Stalks the Harbour? Rabid Gerbil Rampages Through the Streets? Stourhaven was on the Channel coast, no more than a couple of ferry-hours from France; and the Tunnel was not so very far away. There was rabies on the continent—

Rabies. Fever, convulsions, hydrophobia, delirium, and death. Caught from the bite—sometimes the lick—of an infected animal. Incurable.

Sally's hand froze in stroking Kipper's thick black fur. Bouncy, affectionate, hand-licking Kipper. Who might have been dumped. Which for dogs was not unknown.

Any more than it was not unknown for owners who could not—or who would not—have their animals vaccinated and would try to evade Britain's compulsory six-month quarantine period by smuggling their pets through Customs.

CHAPTER TEN

Sally felt sick. Her thoughts were so dismal, and so deep, that she did not hear the receptionist call her the first time. It was only the crisp for-heaven's-sake-are-you-deaf? intonation, clearly the voice of someone tired of wasting her breath on people who did not appreciate her efforts, that succeeded in penetrating the gloom. Was Kipper—sweet little collarless Kipper—a fugitive from justice whose owners could never dare to claim him? It would explain why his loss had not been reported to the police. It would explain how he had become lost in the first place. Raised abroad he would, in the English countryside, with no familiar scents to guide him, have no idea where he was . . .

'I'm sorry,' said Sally as the receptionist glared in her direction. She rose to her feet, squared her shoulders, breathed deeply, and headed with Kipper for the inner door, bound to confess all and to learn her—his—fate. There was no question that she must tell Harry Christopher everything. Other countries, trusting to programmes of inoculation, might live in relative security with rabies endemic in their wild mammal population. Britain had relied for many years on her island status and her quarantine laws. With modern vaccines there had come a slight—a very slight—relaxation of these laws, but even now no animal could enter the country without proper, detailed documentation. Failing acceptable proofs, any animal must be suspect.

Kipper had no papers. He could well be an illegal immigrant. He could have wandered for many miles through the countryside before Sally found him. Her imagination saw harmless, much-loved pets throughout Kent being officially destroyed; saw foxes and squirrels poisoned or shot by the thousand; saw Kipper—

Her hand hesitated on the doorknob. 'That's right,' said the receptionist. 'Through there. Look, do you want to see the vet or not?'

'I'm sorry,' said Sally again. She took one final deep breath, turned the handle, clutched Kipper's makeshift lead in a shaking hand, and pushed open the door.

'You look in worse shape than your dog,' came the greeting from Harry Christopher once the two were safely inside. 'Don't worry—I haven't lost a patient for ages, and this one looks healthy enough. They're tough little beggars, Schipperkes.'

If Sally had only seen the word written down she would have pronounced it 'shipperkers' as she read, but Harry Christopher said 'skipperkees' and later she found out that he was right. The word is Flemish: little captain, little bossy-boots watchdog from the barges of the Low Countries—Belgium, Holland, poppy-red Flanders.

'Sorry?'

He paid her no attention, being busy lifting Kipper—who went at once into his frantic wriggle and kick routine—up on the table. 'You don't see too many of these around,' he remarked as he patted and soothed the little dog. 'In fact I've only ever known one before, and that was . . .'

He stopped. He looked, really looked, at Kipper for the first time; at his head in particular, peering thoughtfully into his strangely blue brown eyes, slipping his fingers inside his mouth, prising his jaws apart. Kipper clamped his jaws together with all the force in his small frame, but it was no use. The vet examined his teeth, then prodded gently at his left hip and nodded as he winced.

'And that was this chap here,' said Harry Christopher. A look of something like disapproval crossed his face. 'Doing Terry Spernall's dirty work for him, are you?'

Sally gasped. She turned pale. Harry stopped glaring at her and released his hold on Kipper to rush round to her side of the table and catch her as she swayed.

'Look, I'm sorry,' he said. 'I should have remembered you weren't well.'

'I—I'm all right,' she told him, doing her best to sound convincing; yet no matter what he might think, she did not convince herself. Delayed shock had suddenly been overtaken by immediate shock. *Terry Spernall's dirty work*, he had said. Terry Spernall's body, lying on Sally's doorstep.

Terry Spernall's dog?

Kipper's claws scrabbled on the smooth rubber surface of the table. In the flurry of trying to stop him plunging to the floor Sally pulled herself together, and Harry Christopher forgot to fuss over her as the little dog ducked and wriggled his head halfway out of the leather belt collar. One pricked ear squashed forwards over the swelling beneath his fur. He yelped with pain, and the shock made it easy for Harry to grab him around the chest as Sally eased the belt back down from the bruised, tender lump.

'There's nothing the matter with me,' said Sally. 'But—his poor head . . .'

'Spernall did this?' Harry Christopher arched one eyebrow and stared at her.

Sally opened her mouth. She closed it without speaking. This was proving more difficult than she had anticipated.

'Well,' said Harry, 'I know my opinion of the man isn't exactly high, but all the same I would never have thought—I'm sorry,' he said again, still holding Kipper in a firm grip. 'That was unprofessional of me.' His smile was now warm, his look no longer cold. 'I do hope you'll forgive the impertinence of the remark.

My personal opinion of Terry Spernall should in no way affect the way I treat his dog. Or . . . his friends.'

The final phrase rang with a faintly questioning note. Sally had no idea how to answer. She could hardly deny all knowledge of Terry Spernall: they had met (if one could call it that) and exchanged words (the same proviso) no more than forty-eight hours ago. 'I think—I think there might have been an accident,' she said in the end.

'Then we'll take a look. Now just you keep still, young Skipper, while . . .'

Of course. Skipper, not Kipper: Skipper the Schipperke. Hardly imaginative, but logical. 'It's okay, Skipper,' said Sally in a reassuring voice, as the vet lightly ran his hands over the little dog's skull and, when the fur rippled across his shoulders, down his spine and each back leg in turn. 'It's all right. You'll be fine . . . Won't he?'

To Sally it was an eternity before Harry Christopher delivered his verdict. 'Well, I can find nothing broken. Not even the skin, though it'll take a few days for the swelling to go down—that's one hell of a bruise, poor chap, but he'll live. Keep him quiet for a few days.' He grinned at Sally, who found herself grinning back. 'Easier said than done, I know, but I don't hold with dosing unless it's really necessary. Which in this case I don't think it is.' He hesitated. 'If . . . either of you is worried

110

about him bring him back, but I should say he'll be his old self within the week.'

Within the week—a week Sally no longer had to wait. Kipper—Skipper—would have no-one to claim him now. Terry Spernall was dead.

'You aren't well,' said Harry Christopher. 'This . . . accident. You were involved, too?' All at once the atmosphere was tense. Even Skipper, who had stopped wriggling now it seemed nothing worse than a few cuddles was going to happen, emitted a queer little gurgle of a growl. 'Look,' said Harry Christopher. 'You can't cover up for him for ever, you know. I think you'd better tell me all about it.'

She told him. Not all, but enough.

'I might have known someone like you wouldn't waste her time on a—sorry.' Another grin, this time embarrassed. 'Shouldn't speak ill of the dead. And I suppose even Spernall must have had his good points, although—' He brought himself up sharply, then caught Sally's eye and grinned again. 'Well, he was the sort of bloke who'd make anyone wonder what the hell his good points might be.' He ruffled Skipper's fur. 'Tried a couple of Alsatians before this young fellow. Got rid of them because he said they cost too much to feed, and it was a bother looking after them.'

The vet's voice hardened. 'Tried to get me to put them to sleep, of all the damnable things.'

111

Sally looked at little Skipper. 'Oh, no.'

'Oh, yes. Wanted a cheaper rate because I'd be doing two together, would you believe? I told him very firmly I had no intention of destroying two perfectly healthy animals to suit his blasted convenience, excuse my French. Offered to rehome them, but he refused my help. Don't know what happened to them in the end. Nice dogs . . . but I grant you they were big. Boisterous. If Spernall had stayed at home a little more . . . His mother was glad to see the back of them, poor woman, so for her sake I didn't ask too many questions I knew I might not like to have answered. She simply couldn't cope with them. She wasn't in the best of health—hadn't been for years.'

Mrs Manchester would be proud of her. Sally asked, very casually, 'His mother's dead now, isn't she?'

'A month or so back.' The vet frowned. 'And then Spernall comes home for the first time in more than a year . . .'

'It can't be a coincidence,' Sally said. 'Can it? They say the solicitors had to advertise for him because nobody knew where he was.'

'Didn't turn up for the inquest, never mind the funeral. The inquest.' Harry Christopher looked at her. 'Adjourned, as I dare say you know.' He paused. 'Another coincidence?'

Sally looked back at him, but had no need to speak.

He nodded. 'Mind you,' he said, trying to

112

rationalise, 'it's not exactly unheard-of to adjourn an inquest. And it doesn't necessarily mean there was anything sinister about it—just that she hadn't seen a doctor for quite a while. Or anyone else,' he added grimly. 'Not even her son, which is another reason I haven't— hadn't—much time for him. The man was an idle drunk and a small-time crook, always in trouble, upsetting the old lady whenever he got caught—and upsetting her even more when he pushed off last year and took young Skipper with him.' Skipper's ears flicked at the sound of his name, but he was still too subdued by being in the presence of a vet to bark and bounce as he had done back at the house.

'Was he Mrs Spernall's dog?'

'No, Terry was within his legal rights, not that he cared tuppence for the law any more than his friends did. As for his family, that was a different kettle of fish—or at any rate his mother was. Her father escaped from Belgium after Dunkirk, married an English girl, had the one daughter and brought her up to be British and proud of it. Which she was. Grateful to England, and said England was good enough for her. Never even had a passport, as far as I know. But she didn't have much luck with the chap she married—a bad lot—and she tried to do her best for Terry, poor woman, once her husband was gone. Scrimped and saved to send him across the Channel more than once to meet what was left of the family. Hoped

113

he'd find a father figure, I suppose.' Harry Christopher shook his head. 'He'll have seen Schipperkes a-plenty there, and they make pretty good watchdogs, if that's what you want—and a type like Terry Spernall obviously felt he needed one—without costing as much to run as an Alsatian. Or a Rottweiler.'

He laughed as he lifted Skipper down from the table. 'Don't tell *him* he's second best, though. Once Mrs Spernall—I mean Terry—got him, I read up about them. You get an awful lot of dog for your money with a Schip.'

'Fifty pounds,' said Sally, recalling the words of Duty Sergeant Biggin: who must have guessed whose dog it was. How else could she explain his conversational pauses? And his insistence that she should consult Harry Christopher rather than risk . . . 'My next-door neighbour,' Sally said, 'isn't a client of yours, is she? Mrs Manchester—Regina Manchester.'

'Josephine,' he said at once. 'Looks like an angel and has worse morals than her mother, though at least she won't suffer the consequences now she's had the op, little devil.' He chuckled, and bent to tug at Skipper's good ear. 'And here's another. You know they call this breed the Little Black Devil? Up to all sorts of mischief from morning till night. No stopping them. You're going to have your hands full if you keep him.'

'A watchdog sounds exactly what I need,'

114

Sally said.

The vet nodded. 'Bark the house down if a leaf drops on the roof, believe me. Never a dull moment. It gave Mrs Spernall a new lease of life when Terry turned up with his lordship here. I went to the house to give him his shots—didn't grudge a home visit, because she found it so hard to get about, though her son could just as well have walked him to the surgery. Better for him, in fact, being the runt of the litter—hips damaged at birth—and the muscle will waste away if he stiffens up and doesn't get regular exercise. You'll have noticed the peculiar way he walks?'

'Sort of hopping at the back,' said Sally.

He nodded again. 'The front has to work twice as hard, and carries most of the weight. That's why he's even more powerful across the shoulders and chest than a normal Schip, from photos I've seen. There's two years of solid muscle built up on those tough little bones.'

'Is that how you recognised him?'

He bent to turn Skipper's face up to Sally's. 'His eyes were the real giveaway: see how they have a bluish tinge, almost like cataract? When he was a puppy the breeder's cat boxed his ears and apparently didn't bother to sheathe her claws. The infection spread too quickly for the local vet to catch it. By the time Terry handed over his five quid or whatever it was, the damage was done. He'll be used to coping with it by now.'

115

He gave Sally a sharp look. 'But how about you? Can you cope?'

'I've never had a dog before—a cat once, but he was run over, and I said never again—but I'll do my best. And my sister-in-law walks Guide Dog puppies.'

'Mm.' He smiled at her. 'That wasn't what I meant, but never mind. For this chap I would recommend dried food and plenty of fresh water, rather than tinned with biscuit . . .'

He gave Sally much advice, a handful of leaflets, and a sample-sized bag of dried food. He told her where to find a pet shop open on Sunday, advising against supermarkets until she had more experience as a dog owner, and told her which collar and lead she should buy. She was to bring Skipper back to have his shots updated after the end of her waiting week 'to save you spending any more than you need right now, just in case anyone does ask about him. Spernall may have had a girlfriend in London, for example. Not that I think they will.' He winked at her. 'Possession is nine-tenths of the law, they say.'

'That's certainly the impression I had when I was talking to Sergeant Biggin.'

'Ah.' Harry nodded. 'A shrewd man, the good sergeant. He doesn't miss much, even though the dog was only in the area a few months before Spernall high-tailed it to London, begging Skipper's pardon.' He patted the little dog's rump, and laughed. 'Did you know Schipperkes are the only breed that can actually be born without a tail? Most are born with, mind you, but they can come out any old length, which is why breeders still like to dock them for . . . uniformity. Can't say I care for it myself. I've seen pictures—jolly little curled-up brushes like a miniature Husky, they are.' As if ashamed of his enthusiasm, he glanced at the surgery clock. 'However, thinking of breeders and their requirements, I'd give this chap his shots this minute, but I'm running late as it is. Settle up with young Tracy outside, and I'll see you again some time after Friday—and you'd better not walk home,' he advised.

He saw her horrified expression. 'I'm sorry, I didn't mean it like that. I was thinking of Skipper. That string doesn't look too strong and I've nothing better to offer, I'm afraid. There's no bus tonight, so get Tracy to phone for a taxi.' Again he saw Sally's horrified expression. 'I'm sure,' he said cheerfully, 'that Rob is more reliable than he looks. Has to be. Otherwise he'd have gone bankrupt years ago.'

And with a laugh and a final pat, he ushered Skipper and Sally from the room.

CHAPTER ELEVEN

It did not take long for the cost of the examination to come through from the surgery computer to the monitor on Tracy's desk, though they had to wait rather longer for the credit card machine to satisfy itself of Sally's bona fides.

'When the line's free I'll call Rob Halliday for you,' said Tracy as the machine grumbled noisily to itself and the paper slip flapped at half mast. 'If Mr Christopher says to have him you'd best do what he says,' she added, at Sally's involuntary wince. 'Honestly, he's not so bad.'

Sally would have preferred rather more enthusiasm in this personal recommendation. Owning a car, she had as yet come no closer to 'Robert Halliday, Luxury Car Hire, Limousine and Taxi Service' than seeing that young man around Stourhaven in a vehicle that looked roadworthy (just) and reasonably clean, but that was hardly luxurious, not a limousine, and not particularly well driven. Of course, he kept the Bentley, the Rolls and the uniformed chauffeur for weddings. And of course the season was only just begun. By the middle of April each Saturday afternoon would find him a vision of gaiters and glittering chrome, of peaked cap and polished buttons and a bonnet with white satin ribbon . . .

The vision faded abruptly ten minutes after Tracy had punched out an automatic number on the desk telephone and with a squeal of brakes Rob Halliday arrived, in jeans and a sweatshirt. But he arrived, which was the main thing.

'Your dog very poorly?' he enquired, as in deference to his weak hip Sally lifted Skipper into the car rather than encourage him to jump. 'Never seen one like that before.' Yes, Harry Christopher had said Skipper was still young when Terry took him away. 'Bitser, is he?'

She thought for a moment, then worked it out: bitser this and bitser that. 'He's a Schipperke.'

'Say again?'

Dutifully she repeated her recent lesson, suspecting she might have to repeat it on many similar occasions if Skipper became legally hers. 'A Schipperke. They were bred as watchdogs—and he's very, very good at it.' There was no harm in letting the word go round that she was no longer alone in the house. 'They come from the Low Countries— Holland, Belgium. The Little Black Devil, he's called.'

The steering wheel jerked in Rob's hands, and his face in the driving mirror was a study. 'Devil, eh?'

'Mischievous,' she quickly explained. 'Lively.

Always into things. Full of himself.' But she could not remember any more, and resolved to return to the library first thing on Monday morning.

'Typical male, eh?' said Rob, with an odd laugh.

'Well, not exactly.' Harry Christopher had confirmed that the little dog's ungendered condition was surgical as opposed to any error of nature. 'Not now,' she said, and this time Rob's laughter was knowing.

'You got company,' he observed, as after a short and mainly silent trip—apart from a muted clunking from the engine and one or two barks from Skipper as he tried to clamber up on the seat and look out of the window—they turned into Sally's road. 'Either you or old mother Manchester, that is. But I'd say it's you they're after.'

Sally would say likewise. She wondered how well the local grapevine worked. When she first gave Rob her name and address, had that been a calculating look in his eye?

'They're after the wrong person,' she said firmly. 'They want Sally Jackson, and I've already told them she's not here.' In the mirror, his eyes met hers. 'She asked me to come and look after the dog for her,' she said, still firm.

'Uh-huh. Fair enough.' Rob drew the taxi into the kerb as close to Sally Jackson's—to the Wellands'—front gate as he could for the cluster of cars and waiting journalists in the road. 'This do you?'

'I think so, thanks—just a minute . . .' She fished in her pocket for her purse, relaxing her hold on Skipper's lead. There was a scrabble and a thump as he clawed his way up on the seat to push past her to the window. He saw the cars; and the journalists. Camera lights began to flash and voices were raised in eager question as he let rip with a series of barks that made Sally's head spin. She grabbed at Skipper, the purse fell to the floor, and she groped around with her free hand as the barks grew fiercer. She bent low, bumped her head, found the purse and dropped Skipper's lead as he leaped and barked and howled at the strangers outside. In the mirror Rob watched the dancing dog and grinned a lopsided grin as Sally rubbed her head.

'Okay, have this one on me!' he yelled above the uproar. 'Get out, quick—and you give 'em hell!'

He seemed to find this remark funny. A warped sense of humour—or a reluctance to be deafened? Or a plain old-fashioned chauvinist lack of chivalry, abandoning a lone female to the media wolves?

The miniature wolf in Sally's arms certainly howled and roared as loud as the real thing. The reporters hoping to crowd her moved hurriedly back as sharp white teeth snapped and the ruff round Skipper's neck fluffed up to make him twice his usual size. He kicked and wriggled, bursting with the desire to roll up his sleeves, spit on his paws and wade right into these trespassers.

'Sally Jackson isn't here!' cried Sally Jackson to the reporters as she dashed through the crowd to the gate, which stood already open. They would have rung the bell, hoping to catch their victim unawares, before deciding to camp outside. 'I don't know when she'll be back! She said to tell you no comment!'

How much of this was audible over the torrent of barking, she had no idea. She did not care. Skipper wriggled and glared and barked over her shoulder as she fumbled with her keys, and not a single reporter dared follow up the path. Sally managed to open the front door and, with Skipper still furious in her arms, vanished thankfully inside.

*   *   *

That night she ignored the blanket box and did not push the chair across the bedroom door, though the giant pepper-mill stayed within reach. But something about the way Skipper snuffled around the house, with frequent growls at the front door, told Sally she would have plenty of warning to deal with any intruders.

At night she fetched her torch, and a longer piece of string. They went into the back garden, where Skipper did what he had to do with the air of a dog who knew his own mind. He rumbled deep in his throat a few times, but his heart was not in it now the reporters appeared to have given up and gone. Sally knew they might be back the following day—but last week's news seldom makes Monday's headlines. With luck they would leave her to enjoy Sunday in peace.

She needed peace: she did not get it. She had found a stout cardboard box, and a blanket she knew could be easily replaced, and put one inside the other in a corner of the bedroom. She inserted Skipper with a goodnight cuddle and a final biscuit, and headed for the bed.

He reached the bed before Sally, stopping his brisk trot a foot or so away to rock back on his hind legs and gather himself for the leap. With a scrabble of paws he was up, sniffing at the pillow, rumpling the quilt, and choosing the exact middle for himself. 'Start as you mean to go on,' Harry Christopher had told her. Sally said No, lifted him off, and put him back in the box.

He got the message. He was very good about staying in the box—until she put the light out. Then it was trot, rock and scrabble, leap, followed by sniff, rumple, and kick as he squeezed as close to her as he could. He had got the message; he made it very clear he intended to ignore it.

And Sally had to admit it was reassuring to have him by her side while she slept . . .

Skipper slept better than Sally did, waking her with a damp thrust of his nose into her face in a manner suggestive of urgency.

'Do you want to go out?'

His ears flicked, and he bounced on all four paws. Out, then. And, after breakfast, a trip to the pet shop for a proper collar and two leads: one short, for pavement work, one expanding so that he could run more or less free in the fields without running away and becoming lost again.

Or hurt. She wondered about that bruise on his head. Had the gallant little scrap tried to tackle his master's killer single-handed? The vet had told her that among his many physical faults Skipper had a badly overshot jaw, but Sally had seen for herself that this did not stop him eating. Biting. Should she tell the police the suspect would probably have a knife in his pocket and badly bitten ankles?

'Nice little chap,' said the man in the pet shop, offering Skipper a biscuit which he snatched and crunched almost in one movement. 'How old is he?'

'Two,' said Sally, and forestalled his next question: 'He's a Schipperke.'

'Is he, now? He's certainly quick,' said the man as Skipper's ears flicked and his blue-brown eyes glittered up at this new friend. 'Not much gets past him, eh?'

'Nothing at all. They were bred as watchdogs . . .'

After the explanation she ran through the list she had compiled with the help of Harry Christopher's leaflets. Collar, lead, two china (stability) bowls (water, food) and a packet of yeast tablets (treats) with a packet of kibble. The plastic bag swung heavily from her hand as she made for home with her dog trotting proudly at her side.

The lone reporter lurking near the house was such a poor hand at an ambush that Skipper's vigorous view-hallooing had him taking to his heels several houses away. Sally saw Mrs Manchester wave from her front window, doing an obvious double-take as she noticed Skipper. Skipper's proud owner waved back, gesturing that she would be across once she had unpacked. Now was the time to see how well Skipper conducted himself when left alone in the house: he might at first sight resemble a cat, but it would take more than a fleeting resemblance for Josephine to accept him as a visitor.

Sally spread newspapers all over the kitchen floor in case of urgent need, and brought the despised cardboard box from the bedroom. She switched on the radio and opened the window: she knew she would hear Skipper raise the alarm if anything happened. She closed the door to the hall, gave him a treat, told him to be a good boy and watch the house for her, and slipped out through the back to the back door of Mrs Manchester's bungalow.

'That is Terry Spernall's dog you have over there,' came the old lady's greeting. 'Is it not?'

Chattery grapevine efficiency. 'Yes,' said Sally.

Mrs Manchester's voice was low, and sad. 'He came looking for him, of course. Tracked him to your door and could find no further trace, poor thing. Dogs are such faithful creatures.' She blinked several times, and there was the suspicion of a sigh before she brightened. 'For myself, I do like a little hint of wickedness to balance things up.' Indeed, Josephine was no angel: and Sally had more than once suspected the old lady of encouraging her.

'These dogs are called Little Black Devils,' she said, launching into what was already her set piece. Mrs Manchester nodded with interest as she listened, settling herself carefully at the kitchen table and motioning her guest towards the kettle and teapot on the side. For the first time she was treating Sally as a friend, not as a visitor. Miss Jackson was flattered.

They sipped their tea and nibbled biscuits as Sally heard the results of her hostess's recent information-gathering.

'His mother was very fond of the dog,' she was told. 'When Terry took him to London it almost broke her heart.' Mrs Manchester sniffed. 'One might argue that he merely finished the job he—and his father before him—had long since started with their—their rackety ways.' Her tone was scornful as well as disgusted. 'Why, the man was more than a—a rogue: he was quite unable to hold his liquor.' Regina Manchester's late husband, Sally knew, could drink like a true gentleman. That epithet was not one she would readily apply to Terry Spernall.

'Of course,' went on the old lady, 'his mother was in a far less robust state of health than I. And Josephine is very little trouble, whereas Mrs Spernall could never have coped with even so small a dog living on her own. It was logical for Terry to take him away, but it was unkind. The poor woman had enjoyed his companionship, you see, because as her son became more . . . disreputable, so she had grown uneasy about furthering close acquaintance with her friends. Having gone through it once with the father it distressed her to realise the son seemed likely to repeat the whole wretched experience. Poor soul, it was not entirely ill-health that made her, towards the end, such a recluse. The dog gave her both company, and an interest in life. And when he went, she started going downhill faster than ever.'

'A year and a half ago.' Sally had done some mental arithmetic in the past hour. 'But surely that can't be why—I mean, she died a month, five weeks back. There simply must be more to it than someone pining for a dog, even if he is the dearest little thing you ever met.' She brought herself up sharply. She must not become a Doggy Bore. 'Does anyone have any real idea of what was behind the inquest adjournment?'

Mrs Manchester shook her head. 'It has been said, and one must take this with a pinch of salt, that the coroner was being cautious because Terry Spernall knew some rather unpleasant people. And he was not the type to play fair.' Bright eyes gazed at Sally in speculation. 'Let us think, my dear. He might well have double-crossed some of these desperadoes—who might have tried to get back at him by hurting his mother—blackmail, you know . . .'

Sally could not decide if this suggestion was being put forward by the amateur detective, or by the would-be writer exploring possibilities of plot. She must be guarded in her reply. Real-life detection was best left to the professionals, but budding writers should always be encouraged. How else would there be fresh books for people to read?

'Mm, yes,' she agreed. 'It could be blackmail—but of course there's more than one sort. Perhaps they threatened his dog, instead of his mother. He must have been fond of him, in his own way. He's such a dear little chap.' She coughed, quickly. 'It would explain why he was so worried that his very last thought was of him. Did you know he was— is—called Skipper? Skipper the Schipperke. And the vet says he needs a special dried diet, not tinned meat. I'm sure that's what he meant. He ate special food. He needed proper looking after . . .'

Again Mrs Manchester sniffed. 'By all accounts it would be the first time that Terry Spernall considered any living creature before himself—and yet you may be right, my dear Sally. As Doctor Johnson might have said, imminent death does concentrate the mind wonderfully. Young Spernall could have regretted his unfilial behaviour regarding the dog and—and tried to make amends in the only way open to him.'

They pondered this in silence for a few minutes. Sally poured more tea from the topped-up pot, but inspiration did not come. She ate another Marie biscuit and wondered how Skipper was behaving himself alone in the kitchen.

'From my reading,' said Mrs Manchester at last, 'I am naturally familiar with the tradition of the crook with the heart of gold.' Her eyes twinkled. 'Or, of course, the tart—do try these lemon curd tarts, my dear.' Meekly, Sally helped herself to one of the proffered pastries. Mrs Manchester cleared her throat. 'It does seem improbable,' the old lady conceded, 'and yet those of us who are closer to the grave than others can appreciate . . .' And a furrow appeared on her brow. 'Schipperke. Ate. Biscuits?'

'But in your book,' said Sally as she subsided, 'there's no reason to leave it that way, unless you want to. 'Quay eight' is so much more—more promising, if we could only know what it promised. Which it still might,' she added. 'After all, we're only guessing at Terry Spernall's state of mind. Perhaps he was every bit as selfish as everyone says and what he said means—well, something else.'

Mrs Manchester's twinkle returned. 'Should it in truth be anything to do with the harbour the police, I am sure, will have discovered it by now. So it will do no harm for others to ask where they have already been. And it will do you no harm, my dear Sally, to take a gentle stroll down there after lunch. Remember, you have to give Skipper's new collar and lead an airing.'

CHAPTER TWELVE

The April shower that had started to fall as Sally hurried back from Mrs Manchester's had long since drifted by. Now the sky was cloudless, the sun bright; the great outdoors beckoned. For the first time with serious intent Miss Jackson slipped the new walking collar over Skipper's head. The scarlet webbing she had thought would make such a handsome contrast disappeared completely into the depths of his ruff. The links of metal chain glinted silver against the rich black of his coat as Sally clipped on his lead, put a few plastic bags in her pocket, made one last check of doors and windows, and then left for the harbour. And—if it existed—for Berth (or Quay) Number Eight.

If it existed. She had tried to tell Mrs Manchester she did not believe it: but in honesty she could not be sure.

'In any case,' said Sally to Skipper, 'the walk will do us good. Come on.'

The little dog trotted merrily by her side, his eyes darting, his ears flicking at each new sound: a car, a crying child, a chirping bird. He was an alert, engaging creature. Skipper the Schipperke, devoted to his master as his master had apparently been devoted to him. And yet . . .

Eight. Ate. Would a dying man really be so concerned for his missing pet's digestion?

Had Terry Spernall's enemies first tried to remove his canine protector by means of poison? A sick watchdog will not bark—or not so loudly as a dog in perfect health. Skipper seemed in perfect health right now, trotting along at Sally's side, pausing to sniff and cock his leg where necessary, ears pricked, eyes bright, and only that peculiar hindquarters hop to warn her if she walked too fast.

'Oh.' She stopped walking as an awful possibility flashed across her mind. Skipper turned to point out that they were nowhere near a lamp post. His blue-brown glare was both indignant and accusing.

Sally laughed, apologised, and moved on. Having worried for several moments she could breathe again. Of course, the delayed poison of her sudden anxious fancy would be worse than useless for a would-be attacker; and if speedy poison had been administered Skipper would have rid himself of it by being sick, in the way of dogs. But any subsequent attack on his master's attackers would have been so feeble they would not have needed to hit him very hard to render those gallant teeth impotent. Sally could imagine the scene. Poor Skipper lay unconscious in the dark as Terry Spernall struggled with his assailants, receiving his mortal wound and fleeing from them through the night—

Bother Mrs Manchester.

But the ideas kept coming.

Them. How many of them? More than one, reasoned Sally. To reach a man's back efficiently with a knife without his raising some objection needed him to be preoccupied at the front. Three men would have finished him off completely. Two men, then—and themselves somewhat damaged in the fight, which damage had stopped them chasing after him at once.

They had followed him from a distance; had seen him reach Sally's—the Wellands'—house; had known the alarm was raised, and had made themselves scarce—

'Ugh.' Sally hoped the men would not come back to find out what Terry had managed to tell her before he died.

She was very glad indeed to have Skipper.

Stourhaven was not a large town. From Chez Welland to the harbour it was just over a mile as the crow flew. As the Schipperke trotted (and sniffed) it took more than half an hour before they reach the first weatherbeaten stones of the West Mole, where the harbour master had his office.

Nobody home. On a quiet and sunny Sunday afternoon in a sleepy, fading fishing port, what else could anyone expect? Sally tried the handle once more for luck, and stood on tiptoe to peer through the window.

Skipper barked, whirled, and threw himself forwards. His lead snapped taut in Sally's hand and pulled her round.

'How do,' said the stranger behind her, with a friendly nod. He was a stout man with a red face, a white beard, and—to complete the patriotic picture—a blue knitted jumper over dark blue trousers. His hands were deep in his trouser pockets, and he had a pipe clenched between his teeth.

'Oh! Hello.' As Sally appeared happy to return the friendly greeting, Skipper gave one

133

last bark and subsided into a suspicious mutter. 'I was looking for the harbour master,' she explained. Burglars, whatever there might be in a harbour office worth stealing, could come in all shapes and sizes—but they seldom took their dogs burgling with them. 'Good boy, Skipper. Good dog.'

'Nice dog,' said the stranger. 'Skipper, eh? Here then, Skipper.' The pipe and the white beard wagged down together as he bent to offer his fist for sniffing. Skipper obliged, sneezed, and lifted his head to be tickled under the chin.

'I'm the chap you want,' said the man, with another nod as he straightened, took his pipe from his mouth and gestured along the pier. 'I take a walk to the end every now and then when the weather's fine. Dropped a couple of lines over earlier, but they don't seem to be biting today.' From his pocket he produced a worn leather case, which he opened to reveal an assortment of keys. With a jangle that had Skipper's ears flicking he applied one of the keys to the office door. 'Never needed to lock this place years ago,' he remarked, ushering Sally before him. 'But we're no more than a couple of hours from London by train, and with the motorway as well there's no stopping the mischief that can be done—ah, and taught, though Stourhaven youngsters are a sensible lot.' He coughed. 'On the whole.'

Sally looked at Skipper, and thought of one

son of Stourhaven who had not been sensible. The harbour master nodded again. 'Albert Biggin told me I'd likely see you around,' he told her. 'Taken quite a fancy to you, he has.'

'I've never met—oh! You mean the dog. Yes, I think he has,' as Skipper wagged his bottom in lieu of a tail and pressed close against Sally's leg, uttering a low rumble when the harbour master moved past her to his desk.

'So what's it all about, then? They tell me you write books about murders. Now, if it's to be smugglers for a change, I could give you enough for a dozen books. And I don't charge for interviews,' he added, with a chuckle that set Skipper rumbling again. 'So long as you spell my name right. They've put me in the papers more than once over the years. Want to see my scrap book?'

Apart from some recollection that Superintendent Groby was involved in an enquiry, Sally had paid little regard to smuggling. Should she have paid more? Stourhaven was a Channel port. No experience was ever wasted, for a writer. Mrs Beeton could take a seaside appointment, for her health, in early spring, after a bad winter had left her prey to enervating chesty colds, despite the vitamin-rich excellence of her cooking. Others would likewise have suffered. As the days grew slowly longer tempers in the household—one of whose members was less than upright in thought, word and deed—

135

would fray. The rough seas of the equinoctial gales would mean that several valuable cargoes were lost . . .

Sally shook her head to muffle the chime of the inspirational bell set ringing by the harbour master's words, then realised inspiration could be adapted. 'Now I know you're willing,' she replied, 'I would love to talk to you, some time when it's convenient. I've never done a book about smugglers, and if you've been written up before it would make the research so much easier if I could use your scrap book for reference.'

'Nothing wrong with right now,' the harbour master said, opening a drawer in his desk. He glanced at her; grinned. He closed the drawer again. 'Can't fool me,' he said, his eyes twinkling. 'That's not really why you came down here, is it? You—and Terry Spernall's dog.'

Sally knew she was no good at prevarication. Honesty was the easiest policy. 'No, not really,' she admitted. 'Mind you, now that you've put the idea in my head it would be a splendid idea for a book. I could talk to you, and take notes—and perhaps you'd let me photocopy your cuttings up at the library.'

'You want to bet?' he said. Only the twinkle in his eye told her there was a joke to be shared, if she would.

'Oh. But—the Grand National's been and gone,' Sally said, after only a moment's hesitation. 'Yesterday.' With so much happening in her life, she had forgotten all about the world's most famous steeplechase.

'Boat Race next week,' said the harbour master promptly, and shut one eye in a long, slow wink. 'So that's settled, then. You come along down with your old notebook and I'll tell you what you want to know. Another day,' he added. 'Of course. So what was it you wanted to know today?'

'How many berths are there in Stourhaven Harbour?'

'Ah,' said the harbour master, bending down to tickle Skipper's chin again. 'For another book, would this be?'

'Not . . . exactly.'

'Didn't think so.' He gave her a decidedly old-fashioned look. 'I've had the police by, asking me the same question—aye, and a bit more besides. Wanted to look at old charts in case it's any way different now to the way it used to be. Which it isn't,' he added, forestalling her. 'Things don't change in Stourhaven. Been numbered berths these I don't know how many years, and so I told 'em. One to twenty-five along each mole, one to twenty the breakwater—as I'm sure you'll find of interest, young lady.'

Meekly, Miss Jackson nodded. The harbour master nodded back, and chuckled. 'Never used letters, as they very well know, excepting E for east and W for west . . .'

She tried to remember just how Terry's gurgling words had sounded. Had she confused 'c' and 'e'? Quay Eight—to sea— Quay 8E . . .

'And the breakwater,' went on her genial host. 'Which is B, of course. East, West, and Breakwater. As if they needed to check! But then that Groby's a terror for routine, as I've no doubt you know.'

'I believe he is,' she murmured, mentally trying out 'b' against 'c' and convincing herself this, too, did not work.

Without warning, the harbour master again took his pipe from between his teeth and with the mouthpiece described a strange and vigorous shape in the air. 'Numbers one to twenty-five, east and west,' he said, and nodded. 'Never nothing else, to which I'd swear my Bible oath if asked—but there's a funny thing, you know. Them and you aren't the only ones to ask me the self-same question, and not so pleased with the answer.'

'Oh?' Skipper's head came up at Sally's tone, but he settled down as he saw that the harbour master had not moved from behind the desk.

'Oh, yes.' Another of those strange shapes was piped vigorously in the air. 'Foreigners, what's more—and no, I don't mean what you're likely thinking, that Stourhaven folk call a man foreign if he hails from the next village, never mind the next county. We see all sorts,

138

here on the coast. Always did, long before that Tunnel and the asylum seekers and so forth. Dutch and French, German and Spanish, Portuguese, Danes, Norwegians. Fishermen blown off course by storms, putting in for repairs, and to feel dry land under their feet again, and to let their families know they've not been drowned.'

He paused, and described one last shape before thrusting the pipe back in his mouth and closing his lips on its stem. He regarded Sally from under beetling brows, waiting with obvious expectation for one who earned her living writing detective stories to make the logical deduction. 'But these—these questioning foreigners,' she ventured, 'weren't any of those?'

'Ah.' The harbour master looked on her with approval. 'No, they weren't. Now I don't have much of what you'd call a schooled education, but this job's an education in itself. You name it, I've seen it—and heard it. And I've never heard nothing like the jabber they were talking together, not unless it was Russian, or Chinese, or one of them other fancy writing sort of tongues a man needs double-jointed tonsils and a dictionary to speak.'

'But they spoke English to you? You understood them?'

'One of them did all the talking, and he wasn't half bad, but his pal never said a word, though I don't doubt we could have worked something out if we'd had to. Like I said, you learn in this job. Not many foreigners I can't get through to in the end, and them to me. Wave our hands a lot sometimes, but we get through. Still, this man—these men—were the same as you and that lad of Groby's, asking about the berths in Stourhaven Harbour. And I told 'em the same as I've told you. And made sure they understood what I was telling.'

Something in his voice alerted her. It had mattered to him that they should understand. 'What sort of people were they?' she asked. 'Fishermen?'

'So they said, but I didn't believe them.' The harbour master frowned. 'A queer pair. Not the sort a man with his head screwed on believes too quickly, though they hadn't the look or the feel of illegal immigrants otherwise I'd have been in touch with the authorities. But there was—well, something about them made me not want 'em hanging around Stourhaven, not when their business ought by rights to have been over and done once they'd learned they must have got the wrong place. And glad I was when they took themselves off this morning, with their funny talk and their queer way of looking—'

'This morning!'

Skipper barked. Sally bent to reassure him. The harbour master removed his pipe from his mouth once more.

'That's right,' he said. 'Three days in a row those foreigners turned up here asking questions—the day after the police, and the day before you. And this morning.' Three times he jabbed his pipe in the air. 'And now they've gone. Which, you may say, is good riddance to a queer coincidence. Only I can't help but wonder what these foreigners might say, if they was to get to hear about it. Because,' he pointed out, 'whoever they are and wherever they come from, this is England. It's a free country. They may well have gone, for the moment. But there's nothing, is there, to stop them coming back?'

CHAPTER THIRTEEN

This was an uncomfortable thought, to which Sally must give due consideration.

Later. Just now she was very happy to chat for a while, learning that her new acquaintance was Jim Tolley. What he didn't know about Stourhaven Harbour (he told her) was not worth the knowing. He couldn't see why young Groby hadn't been able to take his word for it without sending along some poor sprog who had to see for himself. Sally did not like to ask if the sprog under discussion had sported the beginnings of a moustache.

'Talking of seeing,' said Jim, 'there's those

141

lines of mine waiting. Care for a stroll?'

Two of the party strolled, and one of them pattered, to the end of the West Mole to check Jim's fishing lines (still empty) and, coincidentally, to give Sally the chance to see for herself that the mooring berths were indeed numbered one to twenty-five, as they were along the East Mole.

'Shallow draught, lower numbers.' Harbour master Tolley jabbed with his pipe again. 'Bigger boats, higher numbers. Deeper water, see—take a fishing boat, could be drawing twenty foot, and then you got to allow for the tide . . . and the mud.' He sighed. 'Stourhaven's not the place it was. The Stour, it will keep silting up the harbour. There's stuff comes down that river every time it rains, and there's not the money the way there used to be. Once a year, that's all we can afford to dredge now. No wonder so many of these new boating people go further round the coast to one of them posh marinas.'

'Where do the Wellands keep their boat?' Sally asked. 'I'm renting their house,' she explained, though from his quick look she could tell Jim Tolley already knew this.

The harbour master sucked on his pipe. 'They put her in with Ernie Halliday to be laid up for the year,' he said, nodding across the silver lapping sea and the grey stone of the East Mole towards a collection of low wooden sheds on the far shore. 'The Hallidays have always been in what you might call the transport business, one way or another. Rob, he got the cars when old man Halliday died; Ernie, he got the boatyard. They're both of 'em idle blighters, being as they've no competition any more. The town's not half so busy as it used to be, and a lot of folk took their custom elsewhere.'

'Like the boats.'

'The modern ones, most of 'em, yes.'

'But not the Wellands?'

He sucked on his pipe again. 'No,' he agreed. 'Not the Wellands. Fitted in pretty well, they did, for foreigners—in t'other sense than previous,' he added hastily, in case she should misunderstand.

'So when their boat's not laid up with Ernie Halliday, where is she usually moored?'

Jim's pipe stabbed to the eastwards across the silvery harbour. 'Pleasure-boats mostly there, fishing over here—on account of the silting, see. It's got far worse this past winter, with all that rain, and you got to look out for the props. Propellers,' he translated kindly. 'It's a fisherman's livelihood at risk if his engine's fouled with muck stirred up from the floor, whereas for a weekend sailor—' in contemptuous accents—'it's just another letter to the insurance.'

'Any berth in particular?' she pressed on, not wanting to be an impatient landlubber, but needing to know. 'Or would it be first come first served?'

'Not with the fishermen it wouldn't. There's . . . traditions. Superstitions.' He glanced at her—the townie, the sceptic, after a cheap laugh at his expense.

'My parents were both in the Navy during the war,' she said at once. 'My sisters and I grew up knowing what bad luck it was to leave a wineglass ringing.'

He smiled and nodded. 'Yes, and about not putting to sea on a Friday—or if any of the crew's met a woman in white on his way to the ship, or a clergyman. Seafaring folk will never take no more risks than they need—and they'll keep their berths, father to son and beyond.'

'But not the—the pleasure-boats?' The harbour master's contempt for amateur sailors was catching.

'Oh, some like to think they're upholding the old ways, but for them it's just play-acting.' Jim chuckled. 'Mind you, some days, when the weather's fine, there can be more boats than we've got berths, just like in years gone by, with folk dropping in as the fancy takes them from places bigger than Stourhaven, where there's half-a-dozen people to keep an eye on things. But here there's only me—and don't I sometimes know it! Now the Wellands, they're better than most, for they'll go where they're told without argument.' He chuckled again. 'Which is just as well, for they've had 18 E for much of the past year—' he pointed his pipe—

'and with going away they've lost it. When they come back...'

If they came back.

No. She must not think that way.

But. Eighteen E. Eight C. Yes, it was possible. Just. Terry Spernall had slurred those final words...

No. This was something else to which Sally would have to give due consideration. Later. Perhaps while she was walking Skipper round to the East Mole to see—

She had to know. 'Which berth did the foreigners use? The ones who were asking questions?'

'Ah,' said the harbour master, and stroked his beard. 'Now, there's a question. I didn't think anything of at the time, but with them being away for a year...'

'Eighteen E?' guessed Sally, as he paused.

And he nodded.

*   *   *

Skipper and Sally made their way from the West Mole, with Miss Jackson promising to return before too long armed with a thick notebook and a sharpened pencil. A comfortable plot about smugglers would take her mind off what promised to be a most uncomfortable reality.

Yet she had less opportunity to brood than she might have expected. The sun, pale now through a layer of thin cloud, was still bright. The gloss of Skipper's black coat and the little dog's perky demeanour drew admiring looks and interested comments from more than one complete stranger out for the traditional Sunday walk. Some were small children, one or two of whom squealed 'Pussy, pussy,' with enthusiasm, and were very confused when their parents told them otherwise.

Skipper acted like any male animal when surrounded by admirers. The more fuss made of him, the more he played to the gallery; and the gallery was a full one on this first fine afternoon of spring. Sally did not notice whether, among the numerous eyes watching their triumphant progress, there were any whose expression was less admiring than hostile—and not in the sense of simply disliking dogs.

Perhaps she should have done.

Sally meant to go to the police station, but in view of Jim's words she felt it would do no harm to go the long way round. They walked along the sea wall, Skipper garnering squeals and caresses as they went, and reached the shore end of the East Mole. Around the seaward end, Jim had said, the waters of the Stour forever swirled and scoured, dark with their burden of eroded mud and shingle. On a sunny afternoon, from the far side of the harbour, it had not been easy for her to observe this phenomenon properly. Would it

146

waste much more time if, having explored the West Mole, she and Skipper should now investigate its eastern counterpart?

And if in passing they paused to contemplate Berth 18 E, she could not see how anyone could object.

Which nobody did. There was nobody there. Berth 18 on the East Mole was a whitewashed number on a wall, two heavy iron rings set in concrete, and an iron ladder, its uprights a little rusty, with its rungs bright from generations of up-and-downing seaboots.

From the end of the mole Sally gazed down at the turmoil of the freshwater Stour in perennial conflict with the salty English Channel, then back towards Halliday's Boatyard. It was not far. Ten minutes more would never hurt.

She expected to see the double doors of the main shed open and feverish activity within, at this start of the holiday season. There would be coils of rope, and a smell of tar mixed with petrol, that necessary evil. There would be canvas and wood: planks, beams, spars. There would be the sound of hammering, perhaps a cheery whistle or a voice raised in song: a sea-shanty, of course. Ernie Halliday would have a chest and arms muscled from years of physical activity, a mahogany face, and shrewd blue eyes faded from a lifetime's looking out at the proud waters . . .

She saw a low wooden jetty, and a set of

147

metal rails running from the main shed down the shingle beach into the sea. The jetty had several planks either loose, or missing; the rails were pitted with corrosion. The doors from which they ran were firmly closed. The sign above them, announcing that Ernie Halliday had Boats For Hire, on Reasonable Terms, was painted in letters so weathered she had to peer to make them out.

Skipper's ears flicked and his head turned. Sally turned to look with him. A small, wiry man with a crease between his brows and a grubby denim cap on his head was peering back at her from a window in one of the smaller sheds.

'Yes?'

'Mr Halliday?'

'Who's asking?'

Skipper uttered one sharp bark. 'I am,' said Sally.

There was silence. Skipper huffed a bit, but remained still. Sally looked at Denim Cap: he looked at her.

A lifetime of wearing spectacles had its advantages. The short-sighted are so much more used to letting their eyes go out of focus to relax them that they can, if they concentrate, outstare almost anyone.

'Oh,' said the cap at last. It considered the problem for a few moments more, and blinked. 'I'm Ernie Halliday,' it said, with some reluctance.

'I thought you might be,' said Sally cheerily. 'You're looking after the Wellands' motorboat, aren't you?'

'Who says so?'

'Mr Tolley from the harbour.'

There was another silence. 'And what if I am?' demanded Ernie Halliday.

And he had a point. Now that Sally knew, what was she supposed to do with the information?

'I just wondered,' she said, 'whether—anyone—might have come asking for the boat for any reason.'

'I know you,' said Ernie Halliday. Sally was about to protest that as far as she knew they had never met; then she remembered brother Rob, and the taxi-ride home from the vet. Skipper, with his black mane and his tailless machismo, was unmistakable. 'I know you,' said Ernie Halliday. 'You and your devil dog and your damned nosy-parkering. You get out of here and stop poking your nose where it's not wanted!'

And with that he slammed the window shut, and glared at Sally through the rattling glass.

Win some, lose some. Sally had learned her lesson: it would be the peaceful life for her in future. She gave Skipper's lead a gentle tug, and they headed away from the yard and back towards the police station.

This door was open, on such a sunny day. As the pair entered Skipper's claws rattled on

149

the linoleum, and the head of the man at the desk—not Young Moustaches but a beribboned sergeant—came up from whatever he had been doing. His face wore a deep frown of concentration which, after a moment, changed to a long, slow smile.

'Ah, yes. Miss Jackson, isn't it?'

Sally smiled back at him. 'Sergeant Biggin?'

'I am indeed, though you're lucky to catch me today, you and your little dog. Sundays, we like to go round the golf course, me and my old girl. Never miss, normally—but it can't be helped. So this is Kipper, eh?'

The little dog's ears flicked, and he cocked his head to one side. 'Skipper,' said Sally. The sergeant grinned.

'Looks very much at home with you. Do you think you'll be keeping him?'

'Oh, yes. If his owners—if nobody else claims him.'

Sergeant Biggin gave her a capital-letter Look. 'You'll have dropped by to see what news there might be about the incident on Thursday,' he said, as if the rest had been mere courteous exchange. 'Only natural you're interested, being your doorstep and all. Well, I'm breaking no professional confidences when I tell you the deceased has been formally identified as Terrance Kevin Spernall.' Sally found her clutch tightening on Skipper's lead. 'We thought,' said Sergeant Biggin, 'about the dentist, but in the end it was fingerprints we had to use, with him having no next of kin. And no girlfriend,' he added.

Sally's breath—she had not known she was holding it—released in a long, thankful sigh. Skipper barked once, and flicked his ears. Sergeant Biggin went on talking as if the murder investigation was all that must concern his visitor.

'Terry's mother died a while back, though he could only just have found out or he'd have turned up sooner. They lost touch, seemingly, after he made things a bit too hot for himself in these parts and went off to London till they cooled down again. When the solicitors advertised for him, they didn't realise it was still a damned sight too warm for him to come home.' He hesitated. 'And neither did he.'

'Oh,' said Sally. 'You—the police—think he might have met up with some of his—his former friends and they . . . weren't willing to forgive and forget?'

'Something of the sort, yes. Superintendent Groby is having questions asked of one or two local people—but I can't tell you anything about that. Confidential, see.' She saw. She nodded. He smiled. 'It's only natural,' he said again, 'you'd be concerned, having the chap drop dead on your doorstep. You'll be worried about vendettas and so forth. Well, the folk who most likely did for Terry Spernall know their territory. That'll be how they knew he was back in town—and that'll be how they'll

151

know it's nothing to do with you it was your house he came to, just the first in the road.'

'But it's not my house,' she reminded him. 'I'm renting it from some people my husband knows through work.' Should she mention her visit to the harbour?

'The Wellands. Yes.' Was the pause deliberate, or not? 'Yes—but what with the time difference for phoning, and these foreigners having a different idea of police work and no matter how many emails you send you can't force people to answer, well, it's not so easy to check.'

Foreigners again. Sally was about to speak, but Sergeant Biggin hurried on:

'The superintendent's a good man. Doesn't give up. You needn't worry, you and your little dog. You go on home and teach him a few tricks to take your mind off things. My old spaniel, now.' He leaned forwards over the desk to look at Skipper with a Beat This expression on his face. 'Balance a biscuit on the end of her nose and not eat it until I tell her, she can. Sitting up, what's more.'

'The vet—Mr Christopher—says his hips are weak,' said Sally, stifling the further comment that she did not care for tricks with no practical purpose to them. 'I think it might hurt him if I tried anything like that. I've noticed how slowly he has to ease himself down when he sits in the normal way—but teaching him to leave food when he's told is a good idea,' she added, fearing she might have sounded rude. 'On our way here he was hoovering all along the road trying to pick up all sorts of bits of stuff. When the warm weather comes—with flies and things . . .'

The sergeant beamed at her. He, too, was delighted that she was able to make plans for the months ahead: that the little black dog had found a home.

*   *   *

And home they went. The reporters, to Sally's relief, had given up and gone. Next week's news was already on the presses: Terry Spernall and Skipper and Sally M. Jackson were out of time. She was glad.

Josephine was waiting for Sally—and Skipper—when they arrived home. She sat on the gatepost, glaring down with acute suspicion at the black fluffy creature by the side of her friend. The fur rose slowly along her spine, and her tail stiffened from its graceful curve into an angry brush. She stretched forward, sniffed, arched her back, and hissed.

Until that hiss, Skipper had been snuffling happily along with his nose never far from the ground and the lower levels of fences and walls. Now he looked up. He blinked, seemed to focus his eyes, and barked. Josephine hissed again and uttered a curse, scraping her claws

153

across the wooden post and shaving long slivers of oak to the ground. Skipper blinked again as they fell, and examined them in case they should be good to eat. Sally swooped, scooped him up, and carried him kicking and complaining up the garden path.

As soon as she unlocked the door she knew something was wrong. So did Skipper. He stiffened in her arms, and for a moment stopped barking. Together they stood in the hall to feel the draught on their faces—a draught coming from the back of the house, where Sally knew there should have been no door or window open.

The kitchen door slammed shut. The draught vanished.

Sally had closed that door firmly before going out.

She thought about shutting the front door to delay the escape of whoever might still be in the house, then decided to leave it open. Someone her size, with or without a dog, would be crazy to try heroics with an intruder. Anyone now upstairs could make their way outside unnoticed behind her back while she checked the kitchen.

Hazily she recalled a talk once given at CWA, and moved to the side of the hall to walk with care along the edge of the carpet, leaving any footprints down the middle undisturbed. With care she used her elbow to press down the handle of the door she knew

154

she had closed before going out . . .

And saw glass all over the floor from the broken window.

CHAPTER FOURTEEN

Sally stood and stared for a few moments, clutching Skipper close as he wriggled and growled. If he thought she would let him down to tread broken glass into his paws . . .

Anyone upstairs must have heard their arrival. With luck he, she or they would by now have taken advantage of Sally's preoccupation with the kitchen to sneak away. Slowly she turned to look down the hall. She saw nothing move, beyond the rustling branches of the trees outside.

Again she remembered that CWA talk. Pressing close to the wall she made her way from the house and hurried next door. Josephine and Skipper, should they meet, would have to take their chances face to face.

After an eternity of waiting her elderly neighbour came to the door with a smile that was, in the circumstances, ironically inappropriate. 'Sally my dear, what a nice—'

'Mrs Manchester!' Miss Jackson had never been so abrupt with her. 'Look, I'm sorry to bother you, but could I use your telephone? I must ring the police—I've been burgled, and

155

they may have used my phone.' The talk had explained how lazy burglars with a degree of cunning would sometimes use the victim's own phone to arrange their escape by taxi. Sally had no wish to be blamed for having wiped fingerprints from the keys, or for somehow erasing from the memory the last number called.

'Burglars!' Mrs Manchester was at once all sympathy and shocked dismay. Sally regretted having worried her, but hers was the nearest house she could be sure to find anyone at home. The old lady was so disturbed that she paid almost no attention to Skipper, once more on the ground at Sally's side. Perhaps she thought him another Josephine, for she gave him just one quick glance and then beckoned the pair inside without speaking.

'Police, please,' Sally told the operator who replied to her three dialled nines. Mrs Manchester's telephone was in the old-fashioned style that was becoming so fashionable again, though Sally suspected it was not so much a question of retro chic as that at the modernising of the Stourhaven exchange Mrs Manchester would have insisted on the engineers converting her trusty black Bakelite instrument rather than installing any modern push-button monstrosity.

The thought made her smile.

'Police,' said a voice, after another eternity. It was not Sergeant Biggin: he must have sorted out the staffing problems at last and gone thankfully home to his spaniel and their regular, if belated, walk around the golf course. For his sake, Sally was glad. For her own, she wondered if his absence might make explanations rather more difficult.

'I want to report a break-in,' she said, her smile gone. 'I—I've just come home and found the window of the kitchen door smashed and glass all over the floor . . .'

The voice was both practical and brisk. It was even more brisk when Sally identified herself as requested. 'Where are you now?' it demanded, sounding startled. She need not have worried about the difficulties of explaining. Her name and address must have been known to every officer in Stourhaven. 'Next door? Stay there! We'll have someone with you as soon as we can.'

The someone was Superintendent Groby, accompanied by Sally's friend the female sergeant and an earnest young man with spectacles and a large nylon carry-all, bulging with cameras, sticky tape and insufflators. Skipper took the car's arrival as a personal insult. He growled, he roared, he threw himself at the front door and almost pulled Sally's arms from their sockets. She resolved that first thing next morning she would make for the library, and the section on dog training—

No. Not first thing. First, she must have new

glass in her window.

'And new locks on the doors as well,' advised Sergeant Dyer, who had quickly made her peace with Sally's protector by retreating to the garden and offering a now muted Skipper her fingers to sniff. Superintendent Groby loomed in his usual manner in the background, his trousers having passed inspection after several highly fraught moments.

'You'll have kept spare keys somewhere handy, I don't doubt,' he said now. 'Easy for him to find them. They're up to every trick in the book, these devils.'

'Not that he'd get far with this chap on watch,' said Sergeant Dyer, venturing to rub Skipper under the chin. He did not object. 'But you can't stay indoors for ever.'

'Oh,' was all Sally could say. She had not thought so far ahead. The efficient Wellands had indeed left not one, but two spare sets of keys, carefully labelled. Neither set had been hidden anywhere outside: as she knew, burglars were wise to all the tricks, and then more. She had removed the labels from the keys she used every day, but the spares . . .

Sadly, Groby bristled at her. 'You write these tales for a living, Mrs—Miss—Jackson. You've a better idea than many how the minds of these blighters, if they've got minds, work. Now I'm not saying it wasn't a random break-in—with fine weather and open windows it's the same every year—but you didn't have any windows open. So, bearing in mind what happened on Thursday . . .'

'Too much coincidence,' she forced herself to agree, 'is not playing fair with the reader.'

'So my wife tells me. I don't like deliberately scaring people, but I do think you should be careful.'

'Hope for the best,' interposed Sergeant Dyer, 'prepare for the worst, that's the way.'

'We'll board up the window for you before we go,' Groby said, 'and someone'll be round tomorrow about the locks.' He frowned, as if weighing up some important point. He gave a decisive nod. 'Feel up to coming in with us now to see what goes on? It might,' he added, as he saw her hesitate, 'come in handy for one of your books. And we'll need to know what's missing—'

'My new book!' The horror had only just hit her. 'My computer! If he's taken that . . .' Sally always backed up her floppy disk and kept it in another place, but . . . .

'Let's go and see,' said Sergeant Dyer. 'Nice little dog,' she added, as they walked down Mrs Manchester's path with Superintendent Groby close behind. 'Unusual.'

'What's his name?' demanded Groby over Sally's shoulder.

She jumped. There was something in his tone . . . 'I'll give you three guesses,' she said as the party turned in at her gate.

It was the first time she had seen the man even attempt a smile: a poor, creaking effort, but at least he had tried. 'Spot,' he offered, which made Sally laugh, and helped her through the front door before she had time to feel uneasy.

The earnest young man in spectacles had been busy. Sally had written—and read— about it, yet nothing in fiction had quite prepared her for the ubiquitous reality of fingerprint powder. Mrs Beeton's housewifely nature would have been appalled; Sally promised herself an energetic session with the vacuum cleaner as soon as the police had gone. 'My goodness,' she said as she surveyed the scene. There seemed little else to say.

'Goodness? Original sin, more like,' opined the young man in spectacles. Skipper had, in no uncertain terms, given his views on strangers in the house, and by the time everyone had sorted themselves out it seemed foolish to stand on too much ceremony. 'Mind you, you've been lucky. I think there were two of them, sir,' with a nod for the superintendent at her side. Sergeant Dyer was busy with something technical at the other end of the hall. 'But they haven't smashed anything up for sheer devilment the way some of 'em do. Just turned the place over and made off with—well, you tell me,' with a nod for Sally. 'But the small stuff that's easy to fence, at a guess. You can move about now, though I'm not done in the kitchen. Could you give us a rough idea of what they've taken?'

Issuing instructions to his minions as he went, Groby escorted Sally to the sitting room. Skipper grumbled under his breath, although she felt this was more because he was being kept on the lead indoors than because he objected to the superintendent's presence. Once it had sunk in that a friend was a friend, the little dog was willing to allow a certain degree of latitude to others.

'The bureau!' The dark wood was split and white around the lock, which was broken. 'Oh, goodness. What on earth am I going to tell the Wellands? And I've absolutely no idea what's been taken from here,' said Sally, before the superintendent could ask. 'They left it locked when they went, and I don't have a key.'

'It's a few years since I've dealt with this sort of thing first-hand, but I can make an educated guess.' Groby bristled round at the rest of the room. 'You take a good look, and I'll use my initiative.'

She heard him mutter something under his breath—something about he wouldn't be surprised if there was nothing missing at all. If it was meant to reassure, it did not.

'They haven't taken the television or the video.' One of the first things Sally had done on first arrival was to pack away those few ornaments the Wellands had not packed for themselves. Less to dust: less risk of

161

breakages. 'I can't see they've taken anything from in here,' she said, having surveyed the room from floor to ceiling, wall by wall, and back again as she had read Victorian housemaids always did, missing—in theory—nothing. 'Do you think there's anything gone from the bureau?'

'Ha.' Groby rose to his full height, brushing down the knees of his trousers. 'Let's check upstairs,' he said.

Sally did not favour expensive jewellery. She did not want the worry of what might happen when it broke, or was lost. Of her very few pieces most were costume, and those that were not were her wedding and engagement rings, which were safe as ever on the third finger of her left hand.

'They've take a couple of necklaces—one or two brooches—a ring my great-aunt gave me . . .' She closed the lid of the box, feeling slightly sick. She forced herself to look in the direction of the bed.

'And my alarm radio.' It was a relief to find nothing worse had happened. 'That seems to be all.'

'What's in the wardrobe? The chest of drawers?'

'No designer costumes,' she assured him. 'Nearly all my clothes come from charity shops. If it's washable and fits, and the colours are right, I'll buy it. I prefer comfort to high fashion.'

She hesitated, then handed him Skipper's lead while she moved to check—despite her assurances—the wardrobe and four-drawer chest left empty by the Wellands for her use. As she opened each drawer in turn, then checked the garments on hooks and hangers, she could tell that, while all had obviously been disturbed, none of them had been taken. In a way this came as no great surprise. Anyone planning to make easy money by stealing what can be quickly sold on would not help himself to armloads of clothes belonging to someone of small stature. He could have no guarantee of finding a suitable customer fast enough: and if he already had such a customer, he would be stealing to order. And who in his right mind would risk the penalty of the law by stealing what could be picked up at very reasonable cost in second-hand shops all over the country?

Sally found herself smiling. An eccentric, miserly millionairess would fit this particular bill. She wondered what Mrs Beeton would make of it all.

That hint of creative steel was coming through again . . .

The superintendent cleared his throat. Skipper gave a short, sharp bark. Groby spoke quietly. 'You seem happy enough with how things are in here, but we haven't checked the other rooms yet. Is there one in particular where the Wellands put all their valuables and locked the door and left the key with the letting agent?'

'I did the same at my house,' Sally said.

She saw his expression. He already had a shrewd idea what had been going on. And she was beginning to realise.

'This way,' she said, hurrying out without taking Skipper, who dragged Groby in her wake with his claws scuffing the carpet in his haste not to lose sight of her. 'Oh!'

Next to the bathroom was the small spare room, inside which Sally had never seen. It might be Bluebeard's chamber—though she suspected it contained no more sinister items than packed cardboard boxes, a few small pieces of precious furniture, and a rack or two of winter clothes in moth- and dust-proof bags.

Her suspicion had been correct. The hitherto locked and fastened door was locked no longer, and she was able to see inside . . . to see past the splintered wood and scored paint to the chaos of overturned and emptied boxes—of garments ripped from their bags and tossed aside—of drawers upended on the floor, their contents scattered like some bizarre new pattern on the almost invisible carpet.

Groby gave Sally Skipper's lead as the little dog's ruff stood on end, and he growled. 'Well,' remarked the superintendent, 'they haven't smashed the place up, so it could be worse, but they've certainly turned it well and truly over. They were looking for something, Miss Jackson. They weren't what you might call your professional burglars. All those blighters know enough to start at the bottom of a chest to save having to close the drawers as they go.' Yes, she had noticed this—without noticing—in her own room.

'I don't like coincidence any more than you writing lot do,' Groby went on, staring glumly into the wreckage of the spare room with his hands in his pockets, even though the amount of white powder around showed there was now no risk of destroying evidence. 'They didn't seem to have taken anything from the bureau, either. Just a quick rummage, and that was it. Whatever they're looking for, they want it badly.' He looked at Skipper, grumbling at Sally's side.

'I should think you're glad you've got him,' he said.

She was.

CHAPTER FIFTEEN

Four houses down the road lived the owner of Black Tom, ruin of white Persian Badroulbadour, who proved to be a builder. Superintendent Groby persuaded Mr Arnold to defer his Sunday evening television in favour of reglazing the window in Sally's kitchen door.

'They weren't disturbed, so I doubt if they'll be back,' Groby told Sally as Mr Arnold set about his neighbourly good deed. 'There's always the chance they'll try the old putty-hasn't-hardened trick, but my gut feeling is that they had time for a thorough search, so they won't need to bother you again. Either they found what they wanted in the end— or they now know you haven't got it. Take your pick.'

'They took very little,' replied Sally, thinking aloud. 'Just enough to make it look like an ordinary burglary—but they were so . . . thorough.' It was the only word. Untidy, and energetic—and thorough, as Groby himself had remarked. 'Whatever it was they wanted it badly.' She shivered. 'And maybe still do.' It was not a comfortable thought.

'They got away under their own steam,' remarked Sergeant Dyer. Groby looked but said nothing as she gave Sally perhaps more information than Miss Jackson suspected other victims of burglary would routinely be given without asking. Perhaps Mrs Groby had persuaded her husband that people who wrote detective stories were not completely beyond the pale.

'We've checked with Rob Halliday,' went on the sergeant, 'in case they used a mobile to call him—your last number was fine on both phones, Miss Jackson.' Groby snorted. Sergeant

Dyer coughed. 'Rob Halliday says,' she went on, 'that neither of his cars has been to this address—not even this road—since yesterday when he brought you and Sooty here back from the vet.'

'He says,' Groby muttered darkly.

Sally nodded. 'Yes, we walked down to the surgery, but Skipper pulled so much I didn't want to risk it on the way back until he had a proper collar and lead. I suppose I could have driven, but it was such a lovely evening.'

'And his lordship here's an unknown quantity in a car.' Sergeant Dyer was stern. 'He's not exactly a—a calming influence on the ground, is he? You don't want to take any risks with him bouncing about loose in the back.'

She grew sterner. 'Have you any idea of the damage you'd suffer, not to mention him, if you had to slam on the brakes in a hurry? Why people won't wear seat belts in the back is beyond me.' Groby muttered something about fools, but the sergeant ignored him. 'They shoot forward and smash themselves right into the seat in front,' she went on. 'Which is the best way I know of injuring two people at once. There are motorway pile-ups I still have nightmares about, and it's ten years or more since I was Traffic.'

Sally nodded again. 'I thought,' she said, 'I'd see if he would ride under the passenger seat. Or perhaps one of those travelling crates held by a seat belt, only they're quite pricey. Not that I'd grudge the expense if it was necessary, but as it will be Friday before I'm sure I can keep him . . .'

'Only five days to go,' said Superintendent Groby, and managed another creaking smile.

* * *

Clearing up after everyone had gone took longer than Sally expected, and Skipper had to make vigorous representation before it dawned on her that she had forgotten to feed him, the vet having advised that small dogs were better with two small meals a day rather than one large. She made prompt reparation (to him) and a cup of tea (for herself), and took it to the telephone in the hall.

'Mrs Manchester? It's Sally Jackson. Thank you again for having been so kind this afternoon.'

Sally explained most of what had happened, and the old lady well understood that her neighbour had no wish to pop round and tell her in person. 'But if you have time to discuss your theories, my dear, I would be delighted,' she said. 'You may imagine that I have my own theories—but what do you think? You, after all, are the professional.'

'I think the honours in that respect go to Superintendent Groby and Sergeant Dyer. Writing fiction is a lot farther from real life than people imagine.'

'Real life is literally incredible,' said Mrs Manchester, with a chuckle. 'You remember, my dear Sally, that you have told me how on more than one occasion you have had to—to tone down real life because no editor could possibly accept it as fiction.'

This was true. Would a mystery readership swallow the prisoner on remand who, telling watching police that their watching made him nervous, was allowed to close the door of his cell; who used the resultant privacy to saw through the bars of that cell with a hacksaw smuggled in by his wife, and who subsequently made his escape? But it happened, and the newspaper cutting was in Sally's files together with the report of the man who tried to poison his girlfriend with slug pellets (blue) dissolved in her fizzy drink (pink) and was surprised that she noticed. And the gang who used oxy-acetylene torches to break into a dynamite factory . . .

Nobody would accept that a respectable middle-aged crime writer could have a dying man tumble across her doorstep with a cryptic message on his lips. Any wise editor would dismiss it at once as not fictionally credible.

'Well,' said Sally thoughtfully, 'whatever it was they were looking for, it can't have been very small—not sheet-of-paper size, I mean. They poked about in the bureau, but they didn't tip everything on the floor. They must have seen pretty soon that it wasn't in there.'

'But you said,' Mrs Manchester was quick to point out, 'they tipped some of the upstairs drawers on the floor. It was small enough to be buried among clothes, or books packed in boxes. Whatever it was.'

'Not Skipper, at any rate.' No girlfriend would go to such ridiculous lengths to retrieve a dog she had only to knock on Sally's door to claim.

'No, my dear, I believe you may rest easy on that score. Would you like me to have a word with one of my friends on the town council? I feel sure the Pound officials would be willing, in the circumstances, to speed up the legal process of rehousing a stray.'

Sally thanked her neighbour for the offer, but refused it with courtesy. Something superstitious in her nature wanted to play completely fair by the shade of Terry Spernall. She must wait out the full five days before she could feel happy about handing over her fifty pounds to make the dead man's dog her own, and wait those five days she would.

'Then,' said Mrs Manchester, 'we will return to our—to your—mystery. We may take it as read, I suppose, that the burglary is connected to the murder of that young man.'

'The police must think so, or they wouldn't have sent three people to investigate when two would have done. And one of those a superintendent.'

'Just so, my dear. Mr Groby can be a

difficult man, but he is efficient. He would not waste his time. I suppose he gave you no idea of what he thought might be going on?'

He had not, but Mrs Manchester was undeterred. 'Then with no hope of working forwards we must try working backwards. As you tell me you do when you write a book.'

Backwards rather than forwards: yes, it was how Sally plotted, for it was only once she knew, not just who had been killed, but also how, and why, that she could start to work out the red herrings and the various narrative convolutions that were to make Mrs Beeton appear so brilliant when she unravelled them in the final chapter.

But Mrs Beeton was fiction. Terry Spernall was—Terry had been—fact. 'How do you mean, work backwards?' asked Sally, and heard Mrs Manchester sigh.

'That, my dear, was what I rather hoped you might be able to tell me.'

'Real life,' came the reply as Sally thought of Agatha Christie's celebrated Ariadne Oliver, 'is badly plotted, I'm afraid. I can't work backwards, because I've no idea where I'm meant to start working *from*. Writers cheat, you see. We know what the answer is before we begin, and the book is just one way of reaching that answer. Another writer would reach the same answer by a completely different route.'

They discussed the matter backwards,

forwards and upside down for some minutes more, but could reach no sensible conclusion. Reminding Miss Jackson to speak to the insurance company as soon as possible, Mrs Manchester rang off. Sally and Skipper spent the rest of the evening tidying together, and that night she had no qualms about letting him sleep on the bed.

But this time she put the chair under the handle of the bedroom door. Just in case.

*   *   *

Mr Arnold had been unable to fit new locks, but had promised to send someone along as soon as he could the following day. Sally had expected whoever it was to arrive in a tradesman's van: it was therefore a surprise when a Halliday taxi pulled up outside the house.

Skipper let loose what had become the familiar volley of barks, and she fully expected to see the front door buckle before the echoes of the bell died away. She scooped up the dog, held him close, and was kicked firmly in the ribs as she opened the door.

'Hear you've had a spot of bother,' she was greeted by Rob Halliday himself, fortissimo.

She clamped her hand over Skipper's nose. The decibel output was slightly reduced. 'I'm sorry?'

'A break-in. While you was out yesterday

172

with . . .'

'Yes,' she agreed, as Rob jerked his head towards the black furry fury muttering in her arms.

'Need any help? New glass? Mend your locks?'

Sally looked for the bag of tools. It was missing. 'Did Mr Arnold ask you to come? Because . . .'

'Only trying to do you a favour,' he said, as Skipper's back legs flew out with one wild kick from beneath him and Sally had to release his muzzle to catch him as he fell.

'Thank you,' she cried above the noise. 'It's very kind of you, but someone should be along later this morning.'

'That dog,' he told Sally as she regained her balance, 'looks a rare specimen. Little Black Devil, eh?'

'So Mr Christopher told me,' she said. He took a step back as Skipper kicked out again.

'Then I'll be off. Seeing as you don't need no help.' He retreated another step or two, still staring at Sally.

Was he trying to warn her?

If so . . . about what?

She thought again of slow-acting poisons, and of the old friends of Terry Spernall who had apparently taken umbrage at his return. Was a previous friendship with Terry the reason Rob Halliday's name had made Superintendent Groby react in such a grim fashion?

She watched the taxi driver stump off down the path, and had much to ponder as she closed the door on his retreat. Just why had he come to the house that morning? What had he wanted to tell her? To find out?

She would keep a wary eye on Rob Halliday in future.

She hoped the locksmith would arrive soon.

Luckily, she did. Mr Arnold telephoned just before ten to say that his eldest son's wife was on her way, in one of the firm's vans, with an assortment of locks he was sure Sally would find satisfactory. He apologised for not having sent her last night, but he'd seen Miss Jackson had inside bolts on her doors and an excellent watchdog, so he hadn't felt he could interrupt his daughter-in-law's Sunday as well as his own.

'That's all right,' Sally told him. 'It was the glass I was most worried about. Now I've spoken to the insurance company, and they say replacement locks must have . . .' She squinted down at her notes on the telephone pad. 'A deadbolt and at least five levers, if that makes any sense to your daughter-in-law.'

It did. Julie Arnold was a brisk young blonde, wearing a decided air of competence and neat khaki overalls layered with a multitude of tool-rattling pockets. 'I always forget a box is there and trip over it,' she confided, when Sally wondered if she might have been too quick to dismiss the boxless Rob Halliday's offer of help. 'A proper mass of bruises I used to be, before my mum thought of stitching pockets—and I don't leave things behind the way I used to, neither. Now, what sort of locks was it you were wanting?'

Sally always left expert work to experts. She explained what the insurance people had told her and asked Julie to choose whatever she thought best. Young Mrs Arnold made her choice, for form's sake insisting on Sally's approval, and then proceeded to set about her task with energy—and with a small black supervisor. After his initial outburst as the doorbell rang Skipper had calmed down once the young woman was safely inside the house, and then took it upon himself to follow her from room to room doing a Simon Legree on her as she worked.

'Cheeky little devil, isn't he?' Julie seemed amused by his cheek rather than insulted. She reached out a hand to pat him, and he preened himself under her caress.

'He is,' Sally agreed, watching the little dog shove his nose unhindered into several empty pockets, in case they weren't. 'He's a Schipperke,' she said, guessing what must come next. 'A watchdog from the Belgian barges . . .'

Julie's tea-break sandwiches were shared by two, and it was with the greatest difficulty that Skipper was rationed by Sally to crusts only.

His expression as Julie bit into an apple, however, was too much for the lady locksmith. No matter how Miss Jackson protested that he was not starving to death before her very eyes, Mrs Arnold offered him a tasty chunk—which vanished in seconds—when Sally was sure a plain core would have done just as well.

'I wouldn't mind a dog like that,' said the soft-hearted Julie, applying a dab of petroleum jelly to the tip of the last screw to be fitted. 'With him around, never mind the insurance, I reckon you'd have no more need to worry about burglars—though I suppose I shouldn't say that, with being bad for business. We're always glad of the work.'

She did not realise it then, but there would be more work for the firm of Arnold & Sons before the week was out.

CHAPTER SIXTEEN

Sally and Skipper waved Julie on her way, and Sally ate lunch with the shiny new keys beside her on the table and the shining black Schipperke beside her on the floor. The washing-up done and the dishes draining, she slipped the red collar over Skipper's head, checked her pocket for plastic bags, locked the doors and set off for town.

The local bookshop was small, but obliging:

a family business, like so many in Stourhaven. Peter, his daughter Helena and her husband Toby took it in turns to serve behind the counter and to plumb the mysteries of the computer link with the main suppliers' lists.

Sally had to spell it, but she managed to order a book on Schipperkes in particular, buying there and then two books on the training of dogs in general. It had occurred to her that the library was now out as a source of immediate information. Dogs were Not Allowed any more than eating, drinking, or the playing of transistor radios (except in hidden cubby-holes). She and Skipper were still getting acquainted. She felt he would not take kindly to being tethered to one of the outside hooks while she swapped Boat Race forecasts with Miss Gambling Gold Rims indoors.

For the next few days, when not embroiled in the doings of Mrs Beeton (which seemed very tame in comparison with her own) Sally applied herself to the study of responsible dog ownership. She taught Skipper to sit in front of his bowl and leave his food until told he could eat: a major breakthrough for such a greedy little animal, but that fear of poison was not forgotten. She returned to the pet shop and bought a dog harness for use in the car, puzzling for some time over the diagram straps and buckles and their apparent dissimilarity to the real thing. She enquired of Arnold & Sons as to the availability of suitable planks, boards or cut-off bits of fencing that would mean Skipper could have free range of the back garden without going farther afield on some unauthorised expedition.

'I'll drop by this evening to measure you up,' she had been promised; and that promise was kept. Mr Arnold surveyed the gaps in Sally's hedges with a knowledgeable eye, scorning the use of a tape measure.

'We're a bit busy, but I'll sort some stuff for you in a couple of days. You don't need much. I'll get one of the lads to drop it off by the end of the week,' he promised.

'Oh, there's really no need, thank you,' said Sally, not wishing to put him to any more trouble than she had already caused him. 'I can fetch it myself, if you just let me know when. Besides,' as he seemed about to protest, 'it will do the car good to have a run. I've been so busy the past few days it's time it had a proper outing.'

He nodded. 'Yes, you don't want to leave a motor sitting in the garage for too long. We'll tackle most jobs, but a seized-up car's a different kettle of fish from a broken window or a few tiles in the kitchen. You take a trip along the coast and see how your little dog likes playing on a decent beach. Give him a treat, that will.' Stourhaven beach was more shingle than sand, and Mr Arnold was another convert to the Schipperke cause.

It would be a chance to see how Skipper

liked his new harness. Sally removed it again from its wrapping and made comparison with the diagram and accompanying instructions, which in her view were a poor translation by an illiterate Bulgarian from faulty Japanese.

'I think,' she told Skipper, 'that this padded bit goes down your front between your legs—and this loop's a sort of collar back over your shoulders—and this strap is a belt, if dogs have waists. Keep still.'

Skipper decided this was a new game, into which he would enter with enthusiasm. For a dog with problem hips he could certainly wriggle; and his thick ruff was no help. It took several attempts before the buckles were safely buckled, the straps fastened, and—in theory—the harness was ready to be clipped to the human seat belt in the car.

'I'll let you get used to wearing it,' said Sally. 'Five minutes every hour or so should be enough. And if you don't try to claw it off, you can have a treat.'

Yes, she had resorted to bribery: but it did seem to work, and she vowed to cut down on his dinner to ensure he did not grow fat. Harry Christopher had said that an overweight dog was a disgrace, and Sally had no intention of being disgraceful.

It was a dry but overcast day when she reversed the car from the garage and led Skipper, in his smart new harness, out of the house. She opened the passenger door and popped him on the bath-towel she had folded in readiness. She slipped the clip of the belt through the harness loop, snapped the clip in its socket on the floor, and told Skipper to be a good dog while she closed the door and walked to the driver's side of the car.

She opened the driver's door to find a black furry face grinning up at her from the driver's seat.

'How on earth did you—? I suppose the clip must have come undone.' Sally looked at the seat belt: still fastened to its clip on the floor. On the passenger seat, the dog harness drooped limp and empty.

'I did wonder,' she muttered, 'if I'd fitted it right. I'm not sure what went wrong, but . . .'

She went through the whole procedure again. Strap round neck, adjusted to size; buckle fastened. No doubts there. Strap round waist—wriggle, kick; a yeast tablet soothed him, and she buckled him in. She checked the padded webbing round his chest: a snug fit, not too loose, not too tight. He could breathe without suffocating, as he had done quite happily in training about the house.

Once more Sally sat him on the towel, threaded the seat belt through its loop, and clipped it into the socket. She tugged: it stayed. So did Skipper. 'Good boy,' she told him, with a pat. She shut the driver's door, buckled herself into her own belt, and jabbed the keys at the ignition.

A quick black paw flashed out and dashed the keys from her hand. Skipper climbed on Sally's lap and beamed at her. This, he thought, was fun. The best seat, the best view . . .

'You're out of your harness again!' Why does everyone state the obvious all the time? 'You little devil! How did you manage that?'

The third time she was wiser. She buckled and strapped and fastened him in from the passenger side, closed the door—and did not walk round. Instead, she stood and watched in the nearside wing mirror, where he could not see her.

Houdini could have taken lessons. No sooner had Sally apparently left Skipper to his own devices than he performed what could only be described as a gigantic backwards hiccup, straining up and against the tension induced in the belt as he jerked his head sideways and pulled. Like the heroes of old, with one bound the little dog was free.

'I see,' said Sally, very thoughtful. 'I think we had better stop by the pet shop on our way to the builders.'

Skipper behaved very well in the moving car. He hardly bounced at all: but he was a distraction Sally would have preferred to do without, and she resolved that if the harness problem could not be cured he must learn to travel in a basket. She had not forgotten Sergeant Dyer's words about motorway speeding, and she had no wish to become a traffic statistic.

'Ah,' said the man in the pet shop, when she appeared with Skipper (on his lead) and the harness (in her hand) to ask his advice. 'Well now, there's a funny thing. I would never have thought it with a little chap like him, but . . .'

'You mean this has happened before?'

'Once or twice, yes, and always with dogs— in the sense of being male,' as she must have looked puzzled, unable to imagine using a restraint of this type on any of the cats she knew. 'It's been mostly Dobes, lurchers, that sort of thing—deep chest, you see, and the hips nice and trim in the way you don't get with a bitch.'

Dobermann Pinschers and greyhound crosses—dogs built for speed, with a lung capacity any asthmatic would envy. Deep chest, narrow hips—the description fitted Skipper to perfection.

Sally and the pet shop man contemplated the sturdy, slim-hipped little figure sniffing the lid of a container full of biscuits. 'He'd like one of these, I dare say,' said the man, flipping up the lid and inserting a charcoal-coloured bone into jaws already open to receive it. 'Dunno how they manage it, but they kind of wriggle their way out backwards and you can't stop them short of pulling the buckles so tight you'd throttle the poor beggars.' He seemed sorry for Sally. 'Is he a big nuisance when you're driving?'

'I haven't been far with him yet, but I don't want to find out the hard way that he is. And suppose I'm in an accident. I want to know exactly where he is to grab him and get out instead of having to waste time looking for him.' Sally smiled. 'I think swapping my hatchback for an estate just to put bars across the back would be taking responsible dog ownership a bit too far.' She did not add that, while her husband was unlikely to raise any great objection to Skipper, he might very well object if Sally changed the car to which he was, when at home, very attached.

'Wouldn't work anyway,' said the man, still contemplating Skipper, who had once more put on his Poor Starveling act. 'The bars on most of them gates aren't near enough together for the likes of him.' Absently, he offered Skipper another charcoal bone. It was not refused. 'The only answer is a crate or a basket. Cat size'll do you nicely, and a dog as fond of his food as him shouldn't take more than a day or so to get used to being shut inside. How about this?'

Ten minutes later and several tens of pounds poorer (the pet shop offered a trade-in on the harness, but it had not cost much to begin with) Sally left, carrying a handsome grey travelling crate, size one, by the handle through which she would feed the seat belt once it was in its appointed place on the back seat of the car. Skipper trotted along beside her looking both pleased with himself, and full.

*   *   *

Schipperkes are not only rather catlike in appearance: they also have many feline qualities. They enjoy their creature comforts, they have considerable independence of spirit; but their overwhelming curiosity is perhaps the closest similarity of all.

Mr Arnold offered to drop by after work on Friday to see how Sally had coped with the assorted bits and pieces of barricade he and his team had found for her. She thought she had coped, all things considered, rather well. Skipper, literally dogging her footsteps, had followed her from hedge to house and back a score of times or more, tripping her up each time she turned to fetch another of the small planks and boards and bits of trellis she had unloaded from her car and dumped in the front garden. It took three times as long as she had expected it would: which had been no particular surprise to her.

The crucial test came when Josephine, quite as curious as Skipper about Sally's activities, appeared on an overhanging branch of the mulberry tree in Mrs Manchester's back garden. By now Skipper and the cat had confirmed that they were not of the same species. She stared down at him and spat: he bounced up at her and barked. He hurled himself against the amateur handiwork in the hedge, and it held. Sally was pardonably proud of herself.

Mr Arnold, after much head-shaking, allowed in the end that Miss Jackson had not done such a bad job, considering. He altered a couple of boards and a piece of wire trellis for the look of the thing, and took himself supperwards with a final warning that if that didn't keep the little devil in she was to let him know, and he would be round to fix it properly, in a decent light.

In early April the sun sets at around seven. As it was now barely six Sally decided to take these comments as a compliment, and thanked him. He laughed, tickled Skipper under the chin, and went home.

Sally likewise went home, or at least indoors, leaving Skipper to conduct the most thorough investigation of his territory since he had first arrived in search of his late master. His undisputed territory. He was now Sally Jackson's dog: signed, sealed, and delivered that day from the council pound into her care at what she considered a bargain price. Through the kitchen window she kept as watchful an eye on her bargain as any Schipperke would keep on her.

The telephone rang. She looked out of the window. No, she did not yet have that much faith in her handiwork. She called Skipper indoors, and reached the phone just after the answering machine cut in.

It was Mrs Manchester, who spoke breathlessly. 'Sally my dear, I have been waiting for you to finish. I had no wish to interrupt when you were obviously so busy, but I was sure you would want to know. You will simply never guess what has happened.'

'You're right,' Sally said, as Skipper slumped against her ankles in the way she was coming to know. 'Have the police found the men who killed Terry Spernall? Or is there some news about my burglars?'

'Burglars,' echoed Mrs Manchester. 'Yes, that is what has happened, and I feel sure it must be the same people, knowing what you say about coincidence. And this would be far too much of a good thing if it were, so—'

'Mrs Manchester!' She sounded too excited and cheerful to have been burgled herself, and Sally could tell she was longing to be asked. 'Who has been burgled now?'

'Terry Spernall's mother,' said Regina Manchester, in triumph.

CHAPTER SEVENTEEN

'On Wednesday,' she added for good measure, as in silence Miss Jackson absorbed this news. 'They were interrupted by the boy delivering the free newspaper—an honest, reliable boy, I understand, but not especially intelligent. They are told they must put a paper through every letter-box on the round or they will not be paid, and this is therefore what he did, even though he must have known there was nobody in the house to read it.'

Had he not known he must have been about the only person in Stourhaven to be in such ignorance. While Wednesday's free paper covered less news and contained more adverts than the fifty-pence-per-Friday *Stourhaven Chronicle*, it still held several pages of features and articles of interest to a local reader. The report of Mrs Spernall's inquest adjournment was bound to have been given prominence.

'Was he hurt?' Sally asked. Children as young as twelve could be employed to deliver papers—and what twelve-year-old could withstand one, possibly two, hostile adults with every reason to wish their identities to remain unknown?

'He was frightened,' said Mrs Manchester, 'and shaken, of course, but I believe he only suffered cuts and bruises. The foolish child heard sounds within the house, and decided to play detective.' Sally said nothing. 'He went round to the back, saw a broken window, and instead of calling the police made the mistake of trying to peep inside. There were two men, he said.'

'Did he know them? Could he describe them?'

'I understand not.' Mrs Manchester was disapproving. Had the interrogation been left to her, so her tone made very clear, she would have learned more from the paper boy than the police, his parents and the solicitor together. 'It happened so fast, he said. As soon as the burglars spotted him they rushed outside and knocked him down. One of the men tipped all the newspapers on the ground while the other held him captive, and then they tied the bag over his head with the straps, and ran away.'

'Did they escape on foot, or did they have a car?' Sally doubted if they would have risked calling a taxi to a notoriously empty house.

This was something else the chattery hotline had failed to uncover. Mrs Manchester suspected a car at the end of the road, seen but—as is so often the case—unseen by the paper boy as he travelled his regular route. But nobody knew for certain.

'One thing we can probably assume,' Sally said. 'They can't be local. Local villains would know which day the paper was delivered, and at roughly what time. Why run the risk of being disturbed when you don't need to?'

'And locals,' said Mrs Manchester, entering into the spirit of the thing, 'would perhaps have done more to . . . intimidate the boy into not identifying them. They might have hurt him, remember, a great deal more severely than they in fact did.'

188

Sally thought of the harbour master's foreigners. Would an enquiry tomorrow reveal that their boat had once more paid Stourhaven a brief visit on the relevant day?

'Today's Friday,' she said, doing sums in her head. Her own burglary had occurred the previous Sunday afternoon; the foreigners had left their—the Wellands'—mooring at 18E that same morning, Jim Tolley had said. She wondered how far they had gone, and whether they had returned a few hours later not by boat, which Jim would have noticed, but by road. Unnoticed. To burgle her—the Wellands'—house.

And whether they had returned again, having received further instructions, to burgle Mrs Spernall's house some time on Wednesday evening.

And whether they were likely to honour her with their attentions again in—if mental arithmetic had not failed her—one day's time. Tomorrow. Saturday.

She was becoming paranoid. Why should they want to come back? They had already learned there was nothing to find. 'What did they take?' she asked, though prepared to hazard a guess it had not been much.

'Ah,' said Mrs Manchester. 'Yes.' Sally waited for her to go on. 'The man on the beat,' she said at last, 'was told to assist, of course. My dear, I know his mother. I always used to say she should have spanked him much harder when he was a child. I suspect he is more than half asleep most of the time. I would not call him lazy, but . . .'

Her pause was more expressive than an entire paragraph from *Roget's Thesaurus*. 'Which,' she went on, 'is why he remains a constable on the beat, and always will.' That queer little hiccup sounded suspiciously like a suppressed giggle, and it dawned on Sally how most of the intelligence had been acquired. 'It is thought,' said Mrs Manchester in deadpan accents, 'that the villains planned to make off, had they finished their work uninterrupted, with a number of small knick-knacks and ornaments found by the police assembled in the hall.' She paused expectantly.

Sally's professional reputation was at stake. 'For the look of the thing?' she ventured, and heard another giggle.

'So it seems. They had gone through the house in much the same fashion, my dear, as one gathers they went through your own. Everything was overturned in a desperate search for . . . whatever it was they wanted.'

'And still want,' Sally said, feeling slightly sick. 'If they had found it they would have gone straight off with it without wasting time collecting things to make the effort worth their while after all. As it is . . .'

She gulped. 'As it is,' came Mrs Manchester's bracing reminder, 'they have already established to their own satisfaction that you do not have it. They were not, as in the present case, disturbed on the job.' She brought out the slang with considerable pride, and Sally had to smile.

'There is no need,' she was sternly informed, 'to regard yourself as still a—a target, Sally.' Once more there was that note of pride; and once more Miss Jackson had to smile.

'One might,' went on Mrs Manchester bracingly, 'charge you with a hint of self-indulgence—for consider, my dear. Are there not other possibilities than those you now fear? We should accept that coincidence, while of course abhorrent in fictional excess, can happen in fact. The paper boy might have disturbed—dear me—would-be squatters who knew the house was empty, and were frightened off by the boy. Which is why they did not harm him. Hippies, I understand, have a healthy respect for human life, and they are very fond of children.'

Sally hoped they were as fond of adults, but in view of the warning about self-indulgence thought it better to say nothing. To Mrs Manchester it might still be a detective story come alive: but Sally had reached the craven stage of hoping that whoever they were they would not come bothering her again, and was selfishly unconcerned by anything else.

She shivered. Skipper huddled closer on her feet, and she bent to tickle his thick, comforting black ruff. 'By the way,' she said, 'how is Josephine? She doesn't seem too bothered by the way I've blocked the hedge?'

A gentlewoman always follows the conversational lead of another. Mrs Manchester abandoned detection and mystery, and plunged into a lively account of her pet's opinion of planks and boards and bits of trellis across her favourite short cuts. Josephine, it appeared, was sulking. She had turned up her whiskers at kipper fillet, and brought a sad, furry little corpse to bear witness that she suffered such cruel treatment she must fend for herself in the outside world, or be forced to starve.

'Poor Josephine! I'll make my peace with her as soon as I can,' Sally promised. 'Since Skipper came she hasn't had a single one of my digestive biscuits. I'll buy a packet of milk chocolate tomorrow, and shut him away for a while so she can come in. He's learning to be happy on his own, if I leave some toys and it's not for too long.'

'You could bring them round for afternoon tea,' said Mrs Manchester. She knew Sally knew what she meant. 'About half-past two—somewhat earlier than usual, of course, but there are special circumstances, are there not?' And she gave a wicked chuckle which for some reason reminded Sally of Gold Rims in the library.

'The Boat Race?' Sally said, and Mrs

Manchester chuckled again. 'I support Oxford,' she said. Sally told her she was not alone; and hesitated. She would have to leave the house at some time: she could not become a recluse, always on the watch for returning burglars—not with a dog to be walked and a neighbour who was doing her best to convince her there was nothing to worry about.

Sally took a deep breath, and proposed that she and her—or rather Josephine's—chocolate biscuits should arrive some time just after two o'clock, as the outside broadcast began. Mrs Manchester offered to supply throat lozenges, and the pair agreed that they would cheer themselves hoarse as the Dark Blues swept to victory, without once voicing the thought that this year it might be Cambridge who won.

For couch potatoes the Oxford and Cambridge Boat Race is probably the most exhausting of all Britain's country's sporting events, especially on television. The close-ups of the rowers' grim faces, the aerial shots of the thrashing oars of those two eight-legged beetle boats being driven through the water by sheer muscle power, the force of the spray splashing against the camera lens . . . By the end of seventeen or eighteen or nineteen tortuous minutes, the viewer comfortably armchaired at home feels almost as drained as the losers, drooping and broken over their oars while the winners raise the traditional three cheers in voices cracked with emotion.

An understandable emotion. For six months of their lives during the long, bleak winter months, these young men have single-mindedly devoted themselves to the pursuit of physical excellence through diet and training and exercise. Those who try for the teams despair at rejection, and vow to try again; those who make the grade agonise over the possibility of failure in the event itself. No win in after-life is comparable to a win in the Boat Race, no loss less easily brushed aside.

The race is rowed upstream on the tidal reaches of the Thames, from Putney to Mortlake, and the winding course of the river means that, were the teams to row the entire distance neck and neck—which has been known—neither would be handicapped by topography. The Fulham bend at the start, and its Middlesex counterpart at the finish, are balanced en route by the great Surrey bend, equal in length to the other two combined.

For the sake of that initial Fulham advantage it is vital for a cautious cautious captain to win the toss. The choice of station can determine the outcome of the race before a mile is rowed, making the remaining three miles and a quarter no more than a slow agony for those in the boat behind. They, with their backs to those ahead, must fasten their—almost always vain—hope of catching up on their cox, the only one who can see what is happening and do anything about it. His, rarely her, face is a mask. Might he this year perform the miracle of steering achieved only three times in more than a century and a half? His crew cannot tell if his hopes are high, or sunk lower than on that memorable occasion when, tide and weather having combined against them, both boats were overwhelmed, and went down together.

'Cambridge,' came the announcer's voice, 'have won the toss. They've chosen the Surrey station.'

Mrs Manchester sipped her tea. Sally stifled a groan. Surrey was the logical choice for a captain confident in the speed and staying power of his crew. Others preferred the Middlesex station for the early benefit of the Fulham bend. It all rested on how quickly the boats could get away at the start.

'If Oxford can hold them in that first few minutes,' said the announcer, 'they still stand a good chance. Oxford have an overall weight advantage, even if Cambridge have the more experienced crew.'

'I can hardly bear to watch,' said Mrs Manchester, as the boats were directed by the umpire to the stake boats and the ritual removing of pullovers and final flexing of muscles began. 'Oh, dear!'

The upraised arms of the coxes signalled their unreadiness to start. The Cambridge arm went down; the Oxford arm was down—went up again—was finally down.

The umpire gave the signal. The boats powered away from the stake boats with a thunderous thrash of oars, the television informing viewers, after a few moments, that a stroke of 35 was the same for both.

'Oh, dear . . .'

So often it was all over in that first mile; but not this time. The familiar landmarks were passed without one boat pulling more than the odd canvas ahead of the other, which soon regained the inches lost. The commentator reeled off the well-known names. Fulham Football Club. The Mile Post—three minutes and forty seconds for Cambridge, forty-one for Oxford, now stroking 33. Harrods Depository, with its proud Union Flags. Hammersmith Bridge (six minutes and fifty seconds). Cambridge were pulling slightly more than a canvas ahead as they rounded the Surrey Bend into Chiswick Reach . . .

'And half a length ahead as they pass Chiswick Eyot,' came the voice of the announcer. 'This is a really close race!' Sally felt Mrs Manchester shoot a glance in her direction, but could not take her eyes from the screen. 'Oxford,' said the announcer, 'could still do it if they increased the pressure, but . . .'

The suspense was awful. Slowly, slowly the Light Blues pulled ahead, Oxford pressing them every yard of the way, but clearly tiring. When Cambridge swept under Barnes Bridge a length and a half in front, they knew. Barring a miracle, Oxford had lost.

Sally prepared to console Mrs Manchester with the offer of a fresh cup of tea, but found the old lady regarding her with a sparkle in her eyes only that Dark Blue miracle could have justified—and the screen showed there was to be no miracle. 'Sally!' she cried, as the finishing flag was lifted. 'My dear—did you not hear?'

'Hear what?' Sally asked, as the flag fell, Cambridge stopped rowing, and a torrent of cheering erupted. With a cry of irritation Mrs Manchester seized the remote control and plunged her television into darkness.

'It was after Hammersmith Bridge,' she said excitedly. 'Surely you heard? What comes after Hammersmith?'

'Er—Chiswick Steps,' said Sally, racking her jaded brain for the course landmarks.

'Before Chiswick Steps.' Mrs Manchester was trying not to sound impatient. 'Think, my dear. What else is there the announcers always mention?'

Harrods Depository, Hammersmith Bridge, Chiswick Reach, Chiswick Eyot, Chiswick Steps . . .

'Chiswick Eyot,' she said, while Sally was still running through the litany in her head. 'Can you not see? Do you not you hear? Chiswick Eyot . . .'

Eyot: a small island, usually in a river. Alternative spelling, ait. Pronounced ate.

Eight.

The island in the middle of the Stour, not half a mile from where Terry Spernall had died.

CHAPTER EIGHTEEN

'Middle Eyot,' said Mrs Manchester, the sparkle now in her voice as well as her eyes. 'The name may seem illogical in these days when only one remains, but centuries ago there were at least three shingle banks in the Stour. The two smaller have been gradually eroded by the river, and the third grows less with each high tide or heavy rain.'

Sally remembered the harbour master's grumble about the need for frequent dredging, and the swirling silty waters at the seaward end of the East Mole. She nodded. 'You think Terry might have been trying to tell me something about this island? Eyot, I mean. Something,' she hurried on, as Mrs Manchester was about to speak, 'the something everyone has apparently been looking for.'

'That is possible,' conceded Mrs Manchester. A child would have clapped her hands in glee. 'Buried treasure! One *always* finds it on desert islands, of course. And my understanding is that Middle Eyot is as good as deserted. People picnic there in summer,

but after so damp a winter and spring—Oh.'
The sparkle faded. 'I suppose you ought really
to mention this to Superintendent Groby. No
doubt he will wish to instigate a thorough
search.'

'No doubt,' agreed Sally. Then she shook
her head. 'On second thoughts I don't think
so. Won't he have searched it ages ago—for
the smugglers? The ones who were giving him
so much trouble before I came along—that is,
before Terry Spernall. Groby was already
having problems. And he's local, or at least his
officers are. Someone must have thought of
"ate" and "eight" and "eyot"—mustn't they?'

'One would hope so, my dear.' Mrs
Manchester looked uncertain. 'Groby is a
good man, of course, but if he were on the
lookout for contraband, which would be bulky,
he might well pay little or no heed to
something so small the desperadoes believe it
could have been concealed in an ordinary
bureau, or a chest of drawers.'

Sally had to demur. Eagle-eyed Groby
would have noticed anything whatever out of
the ordinary on Middle Eyot, or would have
expected his officers to do so. This was not
high summer, but spring: there would be no
picnic debris to confuse the view. Anything out
of the usual run of seaside flotsam was unlikely
to be overlooked—

'Yes, yes, but—' Mrs Manchester's sparkle
had returned—'what if he searched the island

before Terry's death—and failed to go back there afterwards?' She leaned forward, one gnarled finger raised in emphasis, her voice a thrilling whisper. 'What if nobody has been to the island since?'

Sally made no comment on her hostess's altered timetable: it would have been uncivil to disappoint one whose enthusiasm was so obvious. As was her hinting. So Mrs Manchester wished Miss Jackson to conduct her own search of Middle Eyot—which Sally found it hard to believe Superintendent Groby had not done, if not before, then certainly after, Terry's death. So there could be no harm in it. And Miss Jackson was starting to think she might oblige.

Thinking never hurt anyone, did it?

An excursion to a desert island, even one in fresh water within sight of land, might be fun. Her life, apart from the advent of Skipper, had been little fun in recent days. The exploits of Mrs Beeton were back on schedule: it was, moreover, Saturday. Sally could afford to spare a little time for herself. After all, what else had she to do for the remainder of the day?

But she had no wish to tread on official toes. She would telephone the police station and make enquiry of the affable Sergeant Biggin, who seemed to know all that went on in and around Stourhaven. If he told her there were no objections to her proposed visit—

'Oh,' she said. 'Mrs Manchester, if it's an island, how do I reach it?' Then she laughed; she had the answer before she finished speaking. Her trip to the harbour: her search for the Wellands' motor-boat: Halliday's Boatyard. 'I can row, after a fashion,' she mused aloud. 'Where could I hire a rowing boat at this time of year? Usually, these places don't open until Easter. Ernie Halliday certainly gave the impression last week that he was well and truly closed.'

The old lady chuckled. 'A week is a long time in more than politics, my dear. Besides, from what I know of Ernie Halliday he is not one to miss any chance to make a little unseasonal money by commencing the season rather earlier than the calendar says that it should.' Sally was not so sure. She recalled Ernie's dour expression as he encouraged her off his property.

'The Hallidays are—are individuals,' said Mrs Manchester. It was another instance when an entire thesaurus spoke with less eloquence than a single pause. 'The whole family . . . But I would not advise a rowing boat,' she warned, emerging from whatever reverie Sally's words had inspired. 'The River Stour, so close to the sea, has dangerous currents and undertows. One reads almost every year of a death by drowning, often in boating accidents as rowers become tired and are overturned by the tide. I have read Ernie's advertisements in the local paper. You can drive a car, so the workings of one of the little runabouts he has for hire should not be beyond you—should they?'

She sounded so hopeful Sally found it hard to deny her. Moreover, Mrs Manchester was probably right. In relaxed and carefree mood the average holiday-maker has no time to waste on the study of complex instruction manuals before starting a life on the ocean wave. A motor-boat hired out by Ernie Halliday, brother of Rob, would very likely be a basic ignition/throttle/gear arrangement. As long as Sally kept in mind the rule about driving—or rather boating—on the right rather than the left, all should be well.

She glanced at her watch. 'It can't be far,' she said, half to herself. 'And I could take Skipper. On an island he can run around without his lead, and I needn't worry that he'll take off into the wide blue yonder and not come back. It's high time I practised the Recall over a decent distance—my back garden isn't really a proper test.'

'Indeed it is not.' Mrs Manchester was nodding at Sally over an empty cup, trying hard not to be caught staring in an eager fashion at the sitting room clock. 'I have watched the two of you through my window, my dear. So spirited a little animal as Skipper deserves a change of scene after a week of such intensive training. On so beautiful an afternoon it would be a crime to remain indoors.'

'I suppose they're in the book,' Sally said. 'I could ring to ask if they'd be willing to rent me a boat for an hour or two.' But not, she appended silently, until I've had a word with Sergeant Biggin.

It was Saturday, not near-sacrosanct Sunday, and she was fairly confident that it would be Sergeant Biggin on the desk; and it was. When she explained her interest in a trip to Middle Eyot, and asked if he could think of any reason why she should not go, he laughed and said he could not, and hoped she had a pleasant voyage.

'I thought I might ask Halliday's if they have a boat,' she said. 'But I didn't want to—Well, I just thought I should check with the police first.'

'Mm,' said Sergeant Biggin. 'Hmm.' There was silence on the line for several moments. 'Well,' he said at last, 'if you've doubts about the Hallidays—well, there's that old saying about appearances being deceptive. Their cars may look dodgy, but they aren't—and their boats are seaworthy enough, make no mistake.' Sally could imagine that he had laid a knowing finger against his nose, and winked. 'Very seaworthy, the Halliday boats,' said Sergeant Biggin. 'But I dare say you weren't planning to tell Superintendent Groby about this little trip, were you?'

'If you don't think it's advisable,' she said, 'I

won't.'

'Mm,' he said again. 'Well, we're none of us getting any younger, Miss Jackson, but some of us're worse off for blood pressure than others. No point in upsetting a man more than you need, that's the way I look at it.'

'Me too,' Sally assured him; and winked at the receiver in her hand.

*   *   *

Skipper had already proved himself game for almost anything at any time. Now he merely sneezed at the petrol fumes and allowed himself to be lifted—with those hips Sally thought it unwise to let him jump—without complaint into the small white motor-boat Ernie Halliday, with much grumbling, had uncovered from beneath a heavy tarpaulin she suspected he had only just thrown over it. For something that had lain all winter in the open air round the back of a wooden shed it had acquired a surprisingly thin veneer of dust, dried salt and wind-blown, rotting leaves.

'Two pahnd the ahr and a tenner deposit,' said Ernie, through teeth clamped tight about a roll-your-own gasper. Sally had seldom encountered so virulent a form of tobacco. 'Awright?'

They had already agreed a price over the telephone. From Ernie's expression when he recognised her outside the boatyard Sally suspected he would have doubled that price had he but known in time, and before he could try to bluster she reminded him firmly of the figures quoted. Low-season, two pounds for each hour, plus refundable ten-pound deposit: it did not seem unreasonable. She had asked how long it might take her to travel up-river from the harbour to the island, and he had shuffled a bit before guessing—taking the tide into consideration, and the amount it had of late been raining—an hour should do it easily, there and back.

'And if I overrun,' she told him now, 'of course I don't mind paying extra.' His deep-set eyes lit up under the peak of the grubby denim cap, and he nodded eagerly. 'Shall I check my watch against the clock?' she enquired, innocence personified. 'I assume you go by the one over the harbour master's office, don't you?'

Beside Sally in the boat Skipper grumbled at the muttered curse she pretended not to have heard, though the shower of grey ash was harder to ignore. Ernie scowled across at the small tower on the West Mole, and eventually nodded. 'Ten past, then,' he mumbled. 'From the moment of delivery,' he added, as she was about to protest.

'Quarter past,' she told him, 'from delivery of the keys. I can hardly be expected to use the boat without them.'

With a long, shuddering, ash-sprinkling sigh

and a look of loathing, the key-ring was dropped into her outstretched hand. 'Quarter past,' she repeated, looking again from her watch to the harbour clock and back. 'And if you'll excuse me, time's money. I must be on my way.'

There was hardly any wind, and no especial swell. The Stour estuary, sheltered from the worst weather by the long arm of the East Mole, was easy to reach on a sea whose tide was not flowing strongly. The controls of the little motor-boat were as basic as Sally had expected, and apart from a few backfires to which Skipper responded with barks, the engine ran surprisingly well.

They reached Middle Eyot twenty minutes after they had seen Ernie Halliday stump off back to the ramshackle van in which he had driven to the harbour to meet them. Sally wondered if he would sit smoking and sulking inside until they returned, or whether he would waste fuel and drive home to put his feet up for a lazy three-quarters of an hour or so. She guessed the former, as he was clearly of a saving disposition. She tied a firm knot in her mental handkerchief. The ten pounds she received in due course from Ernie Halliday as a returned deposit had better be the same note she gave him sixty minutes before. She had taken the precaution of noting the serial number before handing it over.

Middle Eyot. Sally turned the wheel, eased

the throttle, and felt like shouting 'Land ho!' but decided against it. Pirates and buried treasure were not serious considerations in her book. She was out for a pleasant afternoon's excursion, with a little safe dog-training thrown in for good measure. They did a slow circumnavigation of the island, which was low and bleak and covered with scrub, and a few scraggy trees. One highly convenient fallen carcase must have dated from a time when the island was larger. It lay now half in and half out of the water, bleached grey above and coated with greenish slime below. Along its weathered length a row of metal rings had been fastened.

'Middle Eyot pier,' she told Skipper, and turned the wheel more sharply. The boat nosed with a juddering crunch into the shingle beach, and Sally gave a couple of quick revs to drive her properly ashore before dragging out the painter from under the board in the bow, and achieving one of her best bowline knots since she and the Girl Guides had parted company more years ago than she cared to remember.

'All ashore,' she said, and hopped out. Before she could turn round Skipper was trying to hop after her, his claws a frantic scrabble in case he missed anything by being left behind. The lead she had tethered to one of the emergency rowlocks to stop him bouncing went taut, and dragged him back. He landed upside down, kicked frantically to right himself, did so with an upwards lunge, and leaped again for the side of the boat.

His paws barely touching the wood, he flew in a single bound over the side. He staggered as he landed on the shingle, shook himself, and rippled his coat over his shoulders. He looked up at Sally as if to tell her how clever he was; Sally looked down at him, and at the collar he was no longer wearing, left behind with the lead on board ship.

'I see,' she said. Skipper flicked his ears and said nothing. 'Yes, very clever, but I don't think we want to go breaking the law, my lad.' She untied the lead and unclipped the collar, putting the one in her left-hand pocket and the other around its owner's neck where it belonged.

Her right-hand pocket held biscuits. She took one and broke it in half. 'Here,' she said. 'This is just to remind you. Behave yourself, now. I don't suppose you'll go too far away, but the minute you start swimming it's back on the lead again.'

Then together they set out to unravel the mystery of Middle Eyot.

CHAPTER NINETEEN

'And what did you find?' Mrs Manchester waited with bated breath on the other end on the telephone.

Sally pulled Skipper's ears gently as he slumped in his favourite position near her feet, glad he had forgiven her for recent ill-usage. She took a sip of tea. 'No buried treasure,' she apologised. 'We looked everywhere for signs of digging, or things having been recently disturbed, but there was nothing like that.'

'But there was something.' Mrs Manchester had caught the note of restraint in Sally's voice. 'Come now, my dear. It is unkind to keep me in suspense.'

'Oh, I don't think it can have anything to do with—with anything. Not really. I mean, you told me people often have picnics on the island. And Ernie Halliday, for all his grumbling and rudeness, didn't seem particularly surprised that I should want to go there.'

'And when you went there?' prompted her neighbour, with a hint of impatience. Sally sighed.

'It sounds daft when you say it out loud. It's just . . . well, the eyot is hardly more than a shingle bank, and very low-lying. When the Stour floods I should think it's almost entirely covered by water. And it's been raining a lot over the past few weeks, hasn't it?'

'Indeed it has. But the river is surely back to its normal level by now?'

'As far as I could judge, yes.' Sally hesitated. 'Of course, shingle drains quickly, and there's barely enough soil to support the trees, such as they are—seedlings from the woods overlooking the river—so the place was hardly knee-deep in mud.' She laughed softly. 'Not human knees, anyway.' The first discovery of Skipper the dauntless explorer had been the one muddy patch on the entire island, across which he had tried to walk without sinking. He did not succeed. A brief dispute ended with Sally frog-marching (dog-marching?) him to a sheltered inlet and sloshing tidal water up his legs to his tummy, which he had regarded as a great indignity. Sally told him she regarded it as even more undignified to risk an argument over her ten pound deposit for the sake of a few brown paw-prints on Ernie Halliday's green and white paint.

Mrs Manchester's laugh was merry. She had Josephine in mind, no doubt, as she said: 'With animals there is never an instant's boredom, my dear. One can never tell what they might do next.'

'What Skipper did,' Sally said, 'was to charge about like a mad thing—what James Herriot's Mrs Pumphrey used to call "going crackerdog". He tore round and round in circles with his legs going in all directions at once, and then . . . well, he tore off in a straight line to a part of the island we hadn't yet reached. And he started rolling in something, so I went to fish him out, and it was . . .'

'Yes?' prompted Mrs Manchester.

'It was bonfire ashes. Fresh ones, from after the last rain. The only damp bits were where Skipper stirred things up. He smelled dreadful,' added Sally, with another sigh. Two sloshings in the river had been followed, once the pair were safely home, by a bath. Only bribery with permitted chocolate drops had convinced the little dog that the shampoo was not dangerous; and once convinced, he had tried to make himself sick by drinking the froth.

'He would,' said Mrs Manchester thoughtfully. 'When it rains after Guy Fawkes Night, the smell . . . But I see what you mean, my dear. So far it has been an unpleasantly wet and chilly spring, with only a few fine days. The weather, in my opinion, is still most unsuited to an outdoor picnic, particularly in such a place as Middle Eyot.'

'In my opinion too,' said Sally. 'I'm a suburbanite at heart. I never enjoyed wholesome outdoor frolics except on the printed page. Camping was the worst part of being a Girl Guide—all that lumpy ground, and the insects, and it was always raining. Fishermen and their families wouldn't be so

211

squeamish, of course—but I would have thought they had better things to do with their time than picnics.'

'So would I, my dear. And smugglers are unlikely to draw attention to themselves by lighting a fire.' Mrs Manchester brightened. 'Might it perhaps have been the police, during their search?'

Sally sounded unsure. 'The state of the ground gave the impression there was more than one person involved—but why would the police light a fire? If one of them fell in the river and got his uniform wet, it would make better sense to dry it properly back at the station.'

'The idea of any police officer so delicate that he is in urgent need of warmth to prevent his catching cold does seem somewhat hard to credit,' agreed Mrs Manchester. 'However. If not smugglers, or the police, or picnickers . . .'

'Children larking about,' decided Sally. 'I've noticed the paper has been coming later than usual in the mornings. It must be the school holidays now and the boy's sleeping in, for which I don't blame him. Children playing Swallows and Amazons, that's who it must have been.'

She tried to speak with conviction, yet Sally could not honestly believe that such traces of a group of youthful Arthur Ransome fans would have given her that uneasy feeling at the back of her neck as she and Skipper explored

Middle Eyot. The sort of feeling in which twenty-first-century logic should not allow her to believe—but which an older instinct warned must result from an unseen watcher, not too far away. The woods overlooking the island loomed, rather than merely stood, on the banks of the Stour, crowding the water's edge. Anyone wishing to remain hidden could do so without great difficulty.

Skipper, intent on exploration, had noticed nothing. There had been no wind to carry scent across the few yards of water: perhaps if there had been, her instinct would have been backed by positive proof.

Not for the first time since her return from Middle Eyot she wondered what her unseen watcher, did he or she exist, might have done more than simply watching, if her watchdog had not been with her.

*   *   *

Next morning the sun shone, the birds chirped, and a story-book spring hovered just around the corner. Nature was a cruel tease. Sally had resolved the night before that her imagination, egged on by Mrs Manchester, was now running a serious risk of getting out of control and must be reined firmly in. Sunday or not, she would quench the fires of self-indulgence by thinking of her contract and devoting herself to Mrs Beeton—but when Sunday came, her heart was no longer in her work. She did her best; but Skipper made it clear he felt neglected, amusing himself by alternately running to the back door to sigh, and gnawing chunks out of a supposedly indestructible polypropylene bone and dropping them just where she wanted to put her feet.

'You need tiring out,' she told him at last, giving in to the inevitable. 'Fresh air and lots of exercise for both of us—but no more imagination, except on paper. I don't want to hear about smugglers, or murders, or burglaries unless they're in the public domain, if that's the phrase I want.'

It probably was not, but Sally did not care. Sunshine made her cheerful. She consulted the Ordnance Survey map and planned a route. She collected biscuits, plastic bags and Skipper's walking gear, secured the house, and set off with the new keys jangling reassuringly on her belt, while Skipper pattered with equal reassurance at her side.

They were going to climb Stour Hill. This was a wooded rise about two miles from the town crowned, according to the map, by an Iron Age fort with earth ramparts and ditch still visible among the trees. It was easily reached along the road until the final quarter of a mile. If, when they came to the lower wood which since the Iron Age had crept up the side of the hill, Sally felt uneasy, they would do a partial circumnavigation (still

214

along the road) of the base of the hill, and then go home again. A walk of five miles in the fresh spring air would do both Skipper and herself no harm, but there was no sense in taking risks.

They headed out of town at a steady pace, Sally's escort pausing at convenient bits of hedge and the poles of signposts to leave his mark. The footpath ran out almost at once, and they walked facing the oncoming traffic, moving close into the hedge as the occasional car drove by. The books might advise holding a dog on one's left at all times, but this was advisable only in countries where they drove on the right.

The road began to climb, and they climbed with it. At the milestone Sally hopped up to look back over the hedge past the curve in the road at Stourhaven below, the sea a glittering grey-blue cloak around its harbour shoulders. She squinted out to sea, but France was lost in a filmy haze. She told herself that perhaps, when she was happy about leaving her dog for longer, she would take that ferry trip across the Channel for some duty-free bargains.

Her dog barked, tugging at his lead. Sally lost her balance and had to jump down from the milestone. Skipper blinked up at her in wide-eyed innocence, his ears flicking. The pair set off again for Stour Hill. It was a beautiful day: the sort of day to make Sally wish she could whistle a happy tune.

They walked on. A passing car slowed to hoot, while the children in the back seat waved and pointed. Skipper took this adulation as no more than his due. Sally waved back, and they walked on again.

From ahead another vehicle was approaching, louder—heavier—than a car, and potentially more dangerous. They pressed into the hedge to wait for it to pass safely by.

The sound of the engine changed. There was a fearsome grinding as the driver crashed his gears, followed by a low rumble. Sally consulted her map: just around the corner they would be near the turning for Stour Hill. The vehicle must belong to the farmer on whose land the fort lay, even though it was not a tractor. A lorry? A large van? Who would deliver to, or collect anything from, the middle of a lonely hilltop wood? A timber merchant?

It might be a bus or a coach, crowded with antiquarians and archaeologists eager to investigate the site of nameless prehistoric rituals—

Sally directed her imagination to stop trying to put a name to even one ritual; and walked on.

At the entrance to the lane up which the non-tractor vehicle had turned, she stopped. She peered through the overhang of trees towards the grey-green distance where she could still hear the engine rumbling as it climbed.

216

'I'd be a fool if I went anywhere near, with all that's been going on recently,' she told Skipper. 'It would be as daft as responding to the anonymous summons to Meet Me At Midnight In The Deserted Church Without Telling Anyone, And Burn This Message Once You Have Read It, by doing just that. People who do deserve everything they get. Which is usually concussion, and sometimes a good deal worse.'

Skipper's ears implied that he agreed with her. Once more she peered up the lane. The engine had stopped.

'We'll cut out the circumnavigation and go home,' Sally told her companion firmly. 'I've retired from the private detective business, remember? And if you breathe a word to Mrs Manchester about the chance I could be missing . . . but then she might say it was too much of a coincidence. Which of course it is. So whatever whoever-it-is is doing, we'll leave them to do it in peace.'

They had gone no more than a few yards back the way they had come when from behind them a sudden strange drumming, clapping sound rose into the air. They turned, Skipper's ears a-flick, to see a dark swirling cloud of grey, white, black and steely blue soar from a metallic gleam near the top of Stour Hill—wheel while it scanned the skies for its direction—and head at great speed out to sea.

As the cloud passed overhead, Skipper

217

barked: probably he had never seen such a sight in his short life before. Sally had. 'Racing pigeons!' Her Hertfordshire home stood not so very far from a railway station where wicker baskets with labels on were often unloaded, taken out to the nearby park, and opened.

Nothing more sinister than racing pigeons. Sally would come to more harm from their feathers (which could make her wheeze) than from their owners, now quietly going about their lawful business by releasing a second basket of birds on what might be a training flight or a race proper, Sally could not tell. Again there came the clap of overhead wings and a few whistling cries as the pigeons headed across the Channel . . .

Towards France.

Duty-free France. Smugglers' heaven.

They would have no barrels of brandy round their necks when they returned, but they might well have—something—strapped to their legs. Sally had read more than one book where precious stones, or lightweight quantities of a mind-altering substance, were carried in lightweight canisters by trained pigeons well beyond the reach of Customs and Excise.

Superintendent Groby had been heavily occupied with smugglers before Terry Spernall expired on Sally's doorstep.

Again she consulted her map. There was a likely footpath about a hundred yards away. She would not skulk her way there behind the hedge: that sort of conspicuous behaviour was always noticed by those with a guilty conscience. She was walking her dog in a public place on a sunny spring afternoon, and that was all.

She found the stile, and with a little manoeuvring of dog and lead and herself—the three of them at one point were trying to go in three different directions—negotiated the way through and over the stile to the path, which ran around the edge of a large field beside a small spinney. Skipper, his ears still flicking as a third batch of birds flew past, barked.

'It's all right. Good dog. They're just birds.'

He barked again and tugged on his lead, thrusting his way through the low grass, his shoulder-muscles rippling. His head was moving from side to side, and his eyes were bright. Sally felt herself getting out of breath as he plunged on, pulling her arm half out of its socket.

She stopped. 'The books say this is bad for both of us,' she told him, wheezing slightly. 'Discipline.' Skipper looked at her, flicked his ears, and barked. Sally stayed where she was. Skipper barked again.

He ducked his head and hiccupped backwards: she was just in time to catch him, but the key-ring on her belt jabbed her in the midriff as she twisted sideways. 'No,' she said, as sternly as she could.

One more cloud of pigeons clapped and drummed across the clear blue sky for France. Skipper barked and ducked again.

This time Sally stood still.

Pigeons, sent by train, labelled in wicker baskets.

Skipper, barking and tugging.

The ache in her side that was not a stitch.

Terry Spernall's dying words.

She stood. She thought.

She looked at Skipper.

'All right,' she told him. 'Lead on.'

CHAPTER TWENTY

The little dog shook himself briskly and got down to business. With his head up he sniffed the air, and let out one quick whimper. He shook himself again, trotted on a few yards and then veered purposefully from the path into the spinney. Again Sally looked over her shoulder. Good. Wherever they were going in such a hurry, it was in the opposite direction from the lorry on Stour Hill.

Some of the trees were in bud, others more sluggish to wake from their winter sleep and greet the spring. Slim green spikes, not yet ready to unfold, speared their way through the moss and dead leaves and dried grass of last year's undergrowth. Pale primroses nestled on the ground beneath a misty gauze of bluebells. The whisper of stubborn winter beech-leaves, still on the branch, was a counterpoint to the snuffles and scuffings of a questing nose and four eager paws.

Skipper seemed to know where he was heading: Sally wished that she did. She cast about in her mind and considered the map she had no time to unfold. How far were they now from her house? Was it in this lonely wood that Terry Spernall—with Skipper—had been attacked? Was the faithful dog, his memory somehow stirred, once more in search of his master?

She knew that she must start searching, too.

But Sally had a better hope of finding what she sought than had poor, short-sighted Skipper . . .

Such a wood, she knew, would have its rabbits, badgers, foxes. Smaller creatures— voles, shrews—might still be hibernating: the warm weather had only just arrived. Sally feared a hungry fox or burrowing badger might have destroyed what she was seeking. As Skipper pulled onward she tried to slow him, her eyes scanning the ground on either side of the path as well as the path itself.

Together they ploughed on through the little wood, Skipper hesitating from time to time but never completely stopping, though his course meandered now, and Sally had time to look about her more closely. She was thankful

221

in more ways than one that this was a clear, bright day in early spring. Lush summer or mellow autumn would have hindered her search both from above, and from below. Through the canopy of budding branches enough sunlight was falling to show up any glint of metal on the ground . . .

Of course, it had rained since then. A splash of mud might cover it.

Would Skipper, with his better sense of smell, be able to find it if her sharper bespectacled eyes could not?

Were they even looking for the same thing?

'Hang on a minute.' Skipper had gone one way around a low bush while Sally, busy looking, had gone the other. The expanding lead gave a horrid buzz, and the automatic rewind was jammed. 'Wait,' she said, going back. She untangled the lead from its twiggy embrace, jiggling the handle a few times before giving it a gentle thump. With a whirr, the lead wound itself into the case again, and they walked on.

She—they—stopped. *Caught on a bush.* Had she been looking in the wrong place all the time? Not on the ground, perhaps hidden in the undergrowth, but a few inches above?

'But I would have seen it shining, wherever it was,' she told herself, hoping this was true.

Caught on a bush. Yes, it was possible: probable, even. After all, Skipper had not managed to find it either. He had been sniffing the ground, not—

He stopped. He sniffed. His head swung round, and he pointed. At the same time Sally saw it too, hanging like a fairground hoop over the sturdy branch of a long-fallen tree close to the ground: a narrow brown circlet with a metallic glitter at its base, a brown snake coiling up from a carpet of moss to strike at the glitter's heart.

Skipper's collar and lead.

'Oh, you poor little thing!' Sally tried to read what must have happened there that fatal night. Terry Spernall, for a reason as yet unknown, had come with Skipper to meet those who were to be his attackers. They disabled the dog by a blow to the head, and callously threw his body to one side. Flying through the air—thirteen pounds of Schipperke will not go far—he must have landed on the trunk of the fallen tree, to roll down and catch his collar over the one branch strong enough to bear his weight as he struggled against slow strangulation . . .

'Oh, that's horrible—you poor little thing!' Sally scooped him up in her arms and gave him an admiring hug. 'But you were so brave—and so clever!'

She had seen him perform his Houdini act more than once; and that Thursday night he must have been desperate. The thick fur around his neck meant his collar did not fit as snugly as it would for a smooth-haired dog. It

223

was why the pet shop man had advised her to buy a combination chain-and-webbing collar (which would close more firmly as the dog pulled) for walks, and to keep the normal circular buckled collar only for indoor use and identification purposes. He had offered her the choice of heart, bone or standard disc shape for engraving with her name and address . . .

Identification purposes. Somehow, Sally did not think the metallic glitter at the base of that collar came only from a disc. She stepped forward to unhook it from the branch. As she touched it, there came a faint jangling sound. One disc by itself does not jangle.

She had been right. A round leather collar, rather worn and weatherbeaten; a lead of plaited leather strips, reminding her of snakeskin. A bone-shaped tag with no name or address, just a telephone number: an owner who wished no one to know who he was, or where he lived.

He might not have been Terry Spernall. Skipper's having come straight to the collar in the middle of the wood might have been pure coincidence . . .

But Sally knew otherwise. There was something else on the collar besides that anonymous bone-shaped tag.

A long, thin key etched with a serial number.

82C.

Neither ate, nor eyot. Terry had said eight—or rather, eighty. Not put to sea, but eighty-two C. Not quay, or Schipperke, but Skipper, key. And Sally thought she knew the key to what.

Had it not been for the pigeons she might never have worked it out. Remembering the birds she had often seen flying from her local park had made her think of the railway staff who obliged by unloading the wicker baskets from the trains. Baskets labelled, for efficient return to their owners, like pieces of luggage.

The Left Luggage lockers on main line stations.

Sally should have rushed back to Stourhaven and told the police—but this discovery was hers. And Skipper's. When Terry Spernall died, the police—as Superintendent Groby had emphasised—had carried out the fullest enquiries. If they failed to enquire as far away as the wood . . .

She should have gone straight to the police. They would probably have cursed her for interfering, but she hoped they would have been grateful for the clue (should it prove to be a clue) even if their failure to find it before Sally did might be slightly embarrassing. If indeed it was a clue. And (if it was) rather more than slightly. The amateur scores over the bungling professionals. Crime Writer Solves Real-Life Murder Mystery—she could envisage the headlines. It would be just as

Groby had predicted when he first spoke to her and had his suspicions aroused . . .

She should have gone to the police. Perhaps, had it not been friendly Sergeant Biggin's day off—'Sundays we always go round the golf course, me and my old girl'—she would have done so. But it was. And she did not.

After all, it might well be no clue at all. She must never forget the possibility of coincidence . . .

They emerged from the wood on the far side, and looked out across the fields.

'I was right,' murmured Sally. A dazed and disoriented Skipper would have found it not impossible, once he regained consciousness and strength, to track his master's fading scent through the rain to the nearest house. To her—to the Wellands'—house. 'Which means,' she told herself with some relief, 'it was just a coincidence after all.'

She estimated the journey would take her around fifteen minutes and resolved to time it, keeping to the edges of fields rather than turning back to use the road. Her uneasy fancy about the pigeon-flyers still lingered, despite her logical deduction that they had nothing to do with the death of Terry Spernall. But Superintendent Groby's smugglers were still, as far as she knew, uncaught.

Skipper's natural perkiness had deserted him for a while, but returned as he moved

226

beside Sally farther from the wood. Something inside him had wanted to go back, but having followed its prompting it was satisfied, and had released him from his obligation to his master's shade. He had a new owner now. His head was up and his ears were pricked as he trotted eagerly along.

'One train an hour on Sundays, isn't it?' Sally checked her watch. 'With luck we could just make the next one.'

It would be a rush, leaving no time for any detour via the police station, or even a telephone call. Which might of course do no more than prove how far she had allowed her imagination to run away with her.

She made up her mind. 'We'll go to London,' she told Skipper. 'And if I'm wrong about all this then nobody—except you—need ever know.'

Sunday walks in the country do not generally require the walker to carry money about his or her person. Sally must go home before catching the train: she must buy a return ticket, and some form of snack—no time for the luxury of a meal at home—and then of course there would be the Left Luggage fee. She assumed Terry had used the Left Luggage at Waterling Cross, which was the terminus for Stourhaven and somewhere she could easily check for herself. If the key did not fit but looked as if it ought to, then she knew she must turn it over to the police, who would know Terry Spernall's full London address and have a better idea of which other stations he might have used.

'I don't know how well you travel on trains,' she said to Skipper, 'but I'm about to find out. If the worst comes to the worst I'll zip you in my bag and carry you.' She had no idea how large whatever-it-was in locker 82C might be, but from the way her burglars had searched she knew it would not be pocket-sized. A dedicated charity shopper and jumble-saler, Sally owned a wide selection of strong nylon bags of varying capacity, into which she could cram a surprising number of books, clothes and little gimmicks for friends.

Plastic bags and a nylon holdall in one pocket; biscuits, her asthma inhaler and her purse in the other, with key 82C concealed in the pocket of her jeans. She had to travel as light as possible—and she expected to be gone for four or five hours at most.

Famous last words? Sally shivered, touched wood, and made her way out through the front door before superstition could start changing her mind.

They had a speedy but uneventful walk to the station. To reverse the car out of the garage, secure Skipper—who had started to bounce as he sensed Sally's growing excitement —and be sure of a convenient parking space at journey's end was an option she considered for only a few moments before rejecting it. There was no time to waste. One or two small children out with their parents wanted to chat and pat but, while Skipper was willing enough, his owner made polite excuses and hurried on. She had no wish to miss this train, catch the next and risk coming home in the dark . . .

Sunday afternoon is a sleepy time in rural England. The station was empty of any officials, but British Rail in its wisdom did its best to provide. Sally fed a ten-pound note into the machine beside the barrier, pressed the appropriate buttons, and received her ticket, her change—and a nasty shock as she heard the shriek of an approaching train.

'Quick!' she cried, wondering how Skipper's short legs would cope with the footbridge steps up, over and down to the far platform. In the event he ran faster than Sally. At one stage in their frantic dash she had visions of tripping over him and both being found at the foot of the steps in a crumpled heap with assorted shattered limbs and two cracked skulls.

The train applied its brakes just as they jumped off the bottom step. Sally looked quickly up and down for an empty No Smoking carriage: it was a non-corridor train, and she had no wish to be stuck with a possible dog hater until the next stop, when convenient or otherwise it would seem very pointed to get out and get straight back in again.

Good. She was almost spoiled for choice. She opened the nearest door, snatched

229

Skipper up, popped him inside, and climbed after him. She sat, breathing hard, by the window, and watched Stourhaven vanish slowly backwards as the train headed for London, and Waterling Cross Left Luggage.

CHAPTER TWENTY-ONE

She was busy catching her breath and congratulating herself for having saved an hour's wait when she realised the central carriage of a London-bound train might not stay empty for the entire journey. The thought of having to spell and explain 'Schipperke' for a possible ninety minutes did not, in Sally's present state, appeal. She was still slightly breathless when the train slowed for the first stop. Too late to decamp with any confidence. She removed her spectacles, leaned hard against the window to assume her most vacant stare, and directed its full off-putting force towards anyone who might think of joining them.

It might have worked, had they been in an end carriage that could only be approached from one direction. As it was they were not, and it did not. Grandad, Grannie and three small boys in baseball caps with the peaks reversed invaded what Sally had hoped would be her privacy—and Skipper's.

The little dog greeted the newcomers with pleasure, and in a merciful silence. He seemed to understand the difference between private and public territory. Sally replaced her glasses and resigned herself to her fate.

'Excuse me mentioning it,' said Grannie once the Oh-what-a-dear-little-dog bit was over, 'but you look a bit peaky, dear. Are you all right?'

'Just a bit puffed, thanks,' said Sally, wheezing as she spoke. 'We had to run for the train, and . . .'

She had spoken carelessly. Never discuss anything personal with strangers. Grannie launched into a horrifying monologue about Her Darren's Youngest, his desperate condition and frequent stays in hospital, and how they'd had to get rid of the cat, and how Sally didn't ought to have a dog if she knew what was good for her, she really didn't.

The little boys (none of whom was Darren's Youngest) voiced shrill and immediate disapproval of this idea. 'But if you don't want to keep him any more, lady, can we have him?' enquired one, more quick-witted than his brothers.

Enough was enough. Sally smiled politely as she took her blue inhaler from her pocket. 'Excuse me, please.' She shook, puffed and inhaled, held for a count of ten, and breathed out. 'I'll be fine in a few minutes,' she said. She had no intention of trying to explain that

231

medical theory held dogs to be a less serious risk to asthmatics than cats. It had been another reason for not replacing her little feline friend when he was run over.

Grannie eventually subsided. The children settled down to play with Skipper, stare out of the windows at the passing scenery, and ask how much longer it was going to be. Sally's heart sank as Grandad's reply revealed that they were going all the way to London.

There's safety in numbers. The thought flashed across her mind and she clutched at Skipper's lead, annoyed with herself. Paranoia was taking hold again. But why—how—should anyone know there was any reason to make her journey unsafe? Dangerous? She and Skipper had been the only passengers to board the train at Stourhaven. Who was following them? Nobody. Grannie and her brood were typical Sunday travellers. As was everyone else on the train . . .

Waterling Cross. They were there. Sally felt a flutter of excitement somewhere inside—or was it hunger? Her blood sugar levels could go up and down in a very unnerving manner, especially when she was under stress. And if the last ten days—if the last two hours—had not been stressful she did not wish to know what was. No wonder Grannie, as they all climbed out of the train and said their farewells, gave her another warning about looking peaky.

'The buffet,' Skipper was told, and Sally was halfway there before she remembered they were unlikely to let him in. Life with a dog was going to be very different from what she was used to. 'Oh well,' she said. 'The book stall, then. They always have chocolate and crisps and things—and we can buy a paper, too. It might be useful camouflage.'

She had no idea from what, or against whom, but she had read too many mysteries where hiding behind a newspaper had been more or less obligatory. If Sally M. Jackson was indeed caught in the middle of a traditional Dying Words detective story, who was she to flout tradition? She bought *The Sunday Broadsheet* and two bars with biscuit and caramel as well as chocolate, then discovered she felt too queasy to eat. She cast a wistful glance towards the station bar, told herself that brandy was less of an answer than willpower, and set about looking for the Left Luggage area.

She could see signs for everything but Left Luggage. Taxis, Underground, Toilets, Tickets—

'Lost, luv?' came a voice that made Skipper spin round, and Sally gasp as she, too, turned and saw a uniformed porter grinning at the two of them.

'Nice little dog,' he observed, as Skipper's ears went flick. 'You waiting for someone, maybe? Or trying to find your way somewhere in particular?'

'The Left Luggage,' she said. He seemed an unlikely spy, and time was pressing. He grinned again.

'People are always asking. Want bigger signs, I keep telling 'em, but do they listen? Nah! I tell you, luv, if I had a pahnd for every time I've told someone where to go—in the nicest possible way, that is—there'd be no need for me to wait another eight years for me pension.'

Sally had no wish to wait even another eight minutes. 'Must I pay you a pound, or does the service come free?' she asked, and the porter chuckled.

'That's a good one, that is. But then anyone as keeps a dog needs a sense of humour—don't they, mate?' He bent to chuck Skipper under the chin, and the little dog seemed to share his amusement. 'You take your missis dahn that-a-way,' said the porter, straightening, and jerking his head with such force that his cap slipped sideways and the peak ended up over one ear. 'And you tell 'em that makes ninety-two lost souls so far this week, awright?'

He was still chuckling at his joke as Sally thanked him and hurried with Skipper towards the sign that, now it had been pointed out, she could see dimly in the distance. Would the desperadoes of Mrs Manchester's imagination have had as much difficulty as Sally in finding their way around? In any well-plotted book they would; but this was real life.

Suppose they had got there first? High-powered desperadoes would know how to pick locks—or how to find someone else who could.

'We'll soon see if the cupboard is bare,' said Sally, as the tall bank of grey metal boxes came into view. 'If it's the right cupboard, that is. And—and the right key.'

She wasted no time in crossing her fingers. She tucked the *Broadsheet* under her arm, gripped Skipper's lead more tightly, warned him to keep his eyes peeled, and began to check the numbering system of Waterling Cross Left Luggage.

The lockers were stacked four high, like a giant club sandwich made of steel. Each layer had its distinguishing letter: A, B, C, D. So far, so good. But if the individual slices were unnumbered, her London trip had been in vain—

It had not.

Numbered they were.

'Oh. My goodness.' Theory was one thing, practice quite another. Sally felt her heart begin to thump as she walked slowly down the line of lockers, offering a silent prayer of thanks that Terry had not chosen to conceal whatever-it-was in Row A. Standing in her shoes little more than five-foot-three she would find it awkward to lift anything heavy from a shelf so high—and this was hardly an

235

occasion when she could ask a bystander for help.

'. . . eighty-one, eighty-two. A, B, C.' As she fumbled in her pocket for the key, Sally looked at Skipper. Did he remember the last time he had been on this selfsame spot? If only he could talk. She looked quickly over her shoulder: nobody within several yards. She looked at the key; at the keyhole; applied one to the other; held her breath.

Then she turned the key. It fitted. After a moment for the tumblers to catch, the locker door swung open.

She reached inside. Something dark, lumpy, dully crackling, in what felt like a nylon bag or holdall similar to the one she had brought with her. Trying to look as if she had simply returned to pick up an item too inconvenient to carry on a previous visit, she pulled at the handle of the bag until it slid forward and she could catch it.

It was heavier than its size suggested. Sally regarded it warily, but it neither exploded nor started ticking. She shook it: nothing rattled, sloshed or oozed. Skipper gave it a quick sniff, but otherwise ignored it: no illegally intriguing smells, then. As something to be found carrying, it should be safe enough. In one respect.

With a little judicious juggling it would fit in Sally's own holdall, which was battleship grey rather than the original dark green: non-newspaper camouflage. She placed her foot on Skipper's lead to restrain him, unzipped her bag, and shuffled the other as far in as it would go, though her estimate had been a little optimistic and the zip would not shut. She folded the *Broadsheet* over the top like a lid: newspaper camouflage, after all.

They were ready to leave.

Or were they? Sally hesitated a moment; then fished out a coin, re-locked the door, and slipped the key back in her pocket. Superintendent Groby would want to see it, she supposed. She had a wild vision of asking him to reimburse her expenses—one railway ticket, one Left Luggage locker—from the petty cash. She giggled.

She shook herself. This was no time for hysteria. Time to catch a train.

The departure board showed that they had ten minutes to wait. She walked Skipper out of the station to a suitable lamp post, and encouraged him to make his presence felt. A taxi driver in the nearby rank hailed them by pip-pipping on the horn, and waving when Sally looked up.

'Oi! Dyed that corgi black, have you?'

'He started off as an Alsatian,' she called through a gap in the queue. 'Only the water was too hot, and he shrank.'

The taxi driver roared with laughter, and Skipper flicked his ears as the queue chuckled and made dear-little-dog noises. Trust a male

237

animal to know when he is the centre of attention. The accusing look he gave when Sally insisted they return inside would have broken a heart of stone: but people who act on impulse should cover their tracks when they can. She had left Stourhaven without letting anyone—meaning Mrs Manchester—know where they were going; partly because of the rush, and partly because it had seemed at the time a little melodramatic to do so.

Now, however, it seemed no more than common sense. The hypothetical Left Luggage had proved to be solid (and fairly heavy) fact. It would be wise to let somebody know where she was, what she had been doing, and when she expected to return. If she could find an unvandalised telephone-box she would do the sensible thing and make a quick call . . .

She found one, and made her call—but it was not quick. Valuable minutes were lost as she waited for Mrs Manchester to hobble to the telephone. Had she known the number for Stourhaven police Sally might, in the circumstances, have risked Groby's wrath, but she did not know it. And to dial nine-nine-nine would have been giving in with a vengeance to paranoia. She gabbled a short explanation— Mrs Manchester was thrilled at what she could understand of Sally's news—and promised to advise the old lady as soon as she could of her safe arrival in Stourhaven.

'And first thing tomorrow,' Sally promised

herself, 'I'm going to buy a mobile phone.'

But tomorrow was some hours away; and she was suddenly hungry. As she headed with Skipper for the indicator board she unwrapped one of her biscuit bars. Two beady blue-brown eyes stared up as she munched. She saved the last, very small, piece to ease her conscience: a glare of such ferocity undiluted for an hour and a half would be more than she could cope with in her present state of mind.

The board said the train was in. They passed through the barrier, the holdall—looped by its handles over Sally's arm as she showed her ticket—bumping against her hip. As well as satisfying her curiosity on this excursion she was going to have a number of interesting bruises to show for it, as well.

Again it was a no-corridor train. She moved to the far end of the platform, where she reasoned weary day trippers would have less energy to walk. Once more she found a No Smoking compartment, climbed in with Skipper, and picked the corner seat with its back to the engine so that she could again try the routine with, or rather without, her glasses. Without them her hand in front of her face was as far as she could see, and the world an out-of-focus blur of moving shapes.

She blinked. She peered.

Two out-of-focus blurs were moving at speed down the platform in her direction.

CHAPTER TWENTY-TWO

She heard a distant whistle, and the clang of a closing gate. The blurs had passed every compartment but this. They paused, dithered, argued briefly, then grabbed the handle, opened the door and jumped in as the train jerked and rattled on its couplings. Departure was imminent—

Was achieved. Sally's glasses were back on her nose, and her companions were no longer out of focus. They looked as charmed by her presence as she was by theirs: a boy and girl, teenagers in love, eager to snatch some time together with no adults to cramp their style. They, like Sally, had hoped for the privacy of the farthest carriage of the train. Now all three must make the best of a bad job: British diffidence made it awkward for either party to leave at the next stop and move elsewhere.

'What a dear little dog!' exclaimed the girl, and even her boyfriend had mellowed by the time Skipper finished wagging his rump and licking every finger within reach.

'He looks hungry,' said the girl, as Skipper sniffed out an empty crisp packet under one of the seats and began to kill it. 'Would he like a biscuit?'

Black ears flicked at the sound of a familiar word. Two sad, starving eyes rolled upwards, showing the whites. At his last gasp, Skipper leaned against the leg of his new friend, too weak to move.

'He's a case, all right.' The boy ruffled Skipper's fur as the third biscuit disappeared. Sally had insisted that it should be the last, but a dog can always hope. 'Wouldn't mind one like this meself—how about you?'

Kelly agreed, and giggled. Sally wondered about suggesting a Schipperke for the wedding list, but did not. Skipper sat panting on the floor, having his chest rubbed. He was still very wary about letting anyone other than Sally touch him from above: that bump on the head was not forgotten.

Kelly and Sam left the train four stops from Stourhaven, vanishing into the mellow privacy of a dusk that had crept up unnoticed during the journey. Sally checked her watch and tried to remember the timetable, as Skipper returned to his long-abandoned crisp packet and set about investigating it for a miracle of crumbs.

She had investigations of her own to pursue, and hoped herself for a minor miracle. If only no-one else got into the train at the next stop . . .

Yet surely there must be time before then for a quick peep. She set the battleship-grey bag beside her on the seat, and pulled off its *Broadsheet* lid. She tugged at the olive nylon inside, and as she tugged felt again that lumpy,

241

dull crackling. Whatever it was had been wrapped in newspaper. Another clue. She knew that different editions held different stories as fresh news came in, and that there were identification marks on the masthead. It had been possible in the past to trace one paper halfway across the country to the individual newsagent who had sold it.

She stopped tugging. She remembered another CWA talk and unfolded the *Broadsheet* so that when the contents of the bag were unwrapped any dust, fibres or similar particles of forensic importance would be collected for future examination.

The olive-green bag stood on its broadsheet safeguard. Skipper gave up disembowelling his worthless cellophane prize and came to see what Sally was doing. She seized the tab of the zip, and pulled. The metal tab grated across the nylon teeth . . . and the zip was open.

'Newspaper,' said Sally, pleased at her guess and somehow not surprised that the typeface indicated a specimen of the tabloid press. The criminal classes, on the whole, were not known for the breadth of their (printable) vocabulary or the depth of their thought processes.

She started to lift out the first of what appeared to be several bundles wrapped in *The Daily Yell*, *The Clamour* or one of their Fleet Street fellows. The holdall wobbled as the train juddered over a set of points, but stayed upright. The bundle was out, and on the newspaper.

Slowly, she unwrapped it.

A gleam of metal. A flash of colour. A heavy clinking as the newspaper fell away . . .

A long and massive chain, intricately worked in dull yellow that surely—surely—could not be gold, its chased and moulded links embellished with gems—with cut-glass brilliants—in blue, red, white, green—with a strange, double-barred cross hanging from the bottom.

'Alloyed brass,' Sally said with a gulp, 'and imitation stones.' She wondered whether she believed herself or not.

Once more she checked her watch. If she was quick . . .

She inspected the second bundle. A small globe of that same dull yellow metal, banded with more bejewelled chasing, and with that same, uncommon cross of double-barred form on what she assumed was the top.

She weighed the globe in her hand. It seemed somehow . . . larger than it really was.

'Nonsense,' she said. She laid it down, and felt the burden of some grave responsibility pass from her.

'Nonsense,' she said again. 'It's imagination, that's all it is.' But she was strangely reluctant to open the third, last, and largest bundle.

She looked out of the window. In the dusk, the lights of an approaching town. The next station could not be far away. If she wanted to know . . .

She did. But she knew there was no time. Everything must be bundled up again as she had found it. Everything for which a man had risked—had lost—his life.

And would any man take that risk for anything less than the real thing?

Sally shivered. 'Talking of lives being at risk,' she said to Skipper as she began rewrapping the chain and the globe, 'with this little lot in our possession I wouldn't exactly say ours were the safest in the world right now. Back in the bag with it all, and fingers crossed until we reach home—and then we go straight to the police, Groby or no Groby. I don't care how annoyed he is. Aren't members of the public supposed to help with enquiries? If only nobody gets in this carriage now . . .'

The train began to slow.

Sally cursed. Enquiries. Directory Enquiries. If only she had thought of this at Waterling Cross . . .

'We'll phone Groby from the station,' she said. 'And ask him to send a car, or an escort, or something. I'm going to feel nervous carting the Ruritanian Crown Jewels through the town, even if I'm sure you'd do your best to protect me.' As she stroked the thick black fur, Skipper licked her hand. 'I don't,' she told him, 'want you hit on the head again. You might not be so lucky a second time.'

Logically, there was no reason whatever

244

that he should be hit on the head; that they should be attacked. Why would anyone know the value of the contents of that innocent grey holdall being carried by an ordinary woman walking her dog?

Logically, there is no reason for travellers to pack passport, tickets and hotel reservations in a secure and convenient place and then to keep checking that place every five minutes, yet they do. Human nature is not logical when it is living on its nerves.

The train stopped: and Sally could have screamed.

'Hey, what a cheeky little devil!' A family of three—fat mother, fatter father, and child of astonishing skinniness—crowded into the compartment with a wicker picnic basket and an assortment of interesting packages. After an initial warning grumble—he had sensed Sally's mood of uncertainty—Skipper was in his element. He batted his eyelashes, wobbled his stump of a bottom, flicked his ears, and implied that if he was not fed within half a minute he would expire at the newcomers' feet.

'Is he hungry? Look at his little face, the imp! You can almost hear him talk. Is it okay to feed him?'

They had succumbed to his charm, and Sally was grateful. His exuberant welcome of the walking larder diverted attention from herself and her grey holdall. She introduced him, explained what he was, how it was spelled. She emphasised that he was a watchdog: the three might seem unlikely spies, but why had they come to the end carriage when one in the middle would have been more convenient? They could have been sent to distract her while the serious ambush was prepared elsewhere. She sat in her corner watching her dog patter freely up and down, and counted the minutes.

Two stops before Stourhaven the family left. Skipper accepted a farewell sandwich crust as compensation for this heartless betrayal; Sally fell to wondering which of the trio (the child had been no more than eight, but cunning knows no age limits) might now be telephoning to alert . . . Someone Else, at Stourhaven.

'Suppose,' she suggested, 'we get out at the next station and ring Groby from there?'

Suppose she could not find a working phone.

Suppose the family had been planted to make her reason in just such a way. Suppose *Someone* was waiting for her not at Stourhaven, but at the less busy earlier stop where—where whatever might be planned could be carried out with far less risk of interruption.

Sally promised herself that never again would she scorn the paranoid workings of a female protagonist's mind.

Why had she gone to the station on foot, for heaven's sake? Why had she not taken her car? His training might be still in the early stages, but surely she could have risked Skipper's bouncing outside the travelling crate for those few minutes before she parked the car?

A parked car can be sabotaged.

And when she set out on her London trip she had been only half convinced it would yield any result.

She must be honest with herself. Less than half. She had not seriously anticipated any trouble.

Had she?

As of that moment she simply had no idea.

'We'll phone Groby the minute we arrive,' she said. 'If there are any—any complications we'll go home for the car. The house is closer than the police station. It should have been safe enough locked in the garage . . .'

She hoped.

CHAPTER TWENTY-THREE

Sally and Skipper were not the only passengers to alight at Stourhaven. A vociferous family of four dropped things, and kept arguing about whose job it was to pick them up, all the way down the platform. Two men in the scruffy anoraks associated with 1960s train spotters or obsessive bird watchers trod purposefully towards the exit in thick-soled shoes. A man with red-rimmed eyes and an overnight bag looked as if he would be very glad to be home.

So would Sally. After her hurried departure for London and her chocolate biscuit bars she was not only hungry, and nervous, but tired. The holdall grew heavier with every step. Skipper was tugging at his lead, eager to reach his supper-bowl. She decided she had had enough.

The disadvantage for anyone travelling in a carriage at either the very front, or the very back, of a train is that of being, on arrival at the destination, at one or other end of the platform, always farthest from the exit. No matter how quickly you walk you will not be first out unless you are the only passenger. By the time Skipper and Sally were at the main door the only working telephone box was already occupied by a tall, thin man with gimlet eyes and an air of intense exasperation as he dialled number after number that apparently went unanswered.

Paranoia shrieked that he had been planted to prevent her calling the police before—before Something could happen.

Sally had no plans to wait around until it did.

A cheap day return ticket, plus two bars of chocolate and a Left Luggage locker, had taken all but a few coins of the modest sum with which Sally had started out. The burglary had made her wary about keeping too much money in the house when she was unlikely to need it. She seldom went shopping on Sundays: she had planned to take more out of the cash machine during Monday afternoon's walk.

She left the station to find Rob Halliday's taxi in its usual place. He was doing his best to read a newspaper in the twilight no British Rail lamp had as yet relieved. She wondered what he would say if she asked him to drive her to the police station.

She wondered what Superintendent Groby would say if she asked him to pay her taxi.

Suppose Groby, like Sergeant Biggin, was not on duty? Would anyone else be likely to believe that the contents of Sally's holdall might be worth a king's ransom . . . when she did not know if she seriously believed it herself?

'Taxi?' Rob threw his paper on the seat beside him, and jerked his head. 'Take you home?'

The idea seemed suddenly very appealing.

'You'll have to trust me for the money,' she warned him, 'until we get there, if that's all right.'

'Swap you for the dog,' he offered with a flash of teeth to show, she imagined, that it was meant to be a joke.

'I'll put you on the waiting-list,' she said. 'At about number eight—er—eighteen, the last time I counted.' At least she had not said eighty-two C.

'Hop in.' He leaned back over the driver's seat to open the passenger door. Thankfully she swung the holdall inside as Skipper did his funny little scrabbling vault and landed beside it on the floor. Sally followed, flexing her carrying arm and promising herself a hot bath before she was much older.

After she had fed Skipper, of course.

After she had found out what else was in the holdall . . .

'Belt on?' Rob might, according to gossip, be an erratic personality, but he seemed willing to uphold the visible law (if that was the phrase) no matter how doubtful his reputation in other directions. He checked in the mirror, nodded, and started the car.

'Been to London, have you?'

'Just a quick trip.' Sally crossed mental fingers: it was not strictly true. 'I don't altogether hold with Sunday shopping, but sometimes . . .'

She left the sentence unfinished, hoping he would make the right—or rather, wrong—assumption.

'Funny to take a dog shopping,' he observed.

'Oh—well, yes, but he's so small I can carry him if people make a fuss. And really, they

250

hardly notice him, and when they do they don't seem to mind. Quite the reverse, in fact.'

'Casts a spell on 'em, does he?' Rob chuckled. 'That's some dog you've got yourself there, all right.'

'I know,' Sally said, as Skipper's ears flicked and he began to bounce. 'Steady, boy!' She thrust her foot sideways and clamped it on the webbing part of his lead, pulling him gently to the floor until he was still.

He gave her a reproachful look, and she patted him as he subsided, telling him he was a good dog, and thinking that they made a fine pair—she in her inertia seatbelt, and Skipper with his expanding lead. A good team. 'Good dog,' she said again. 'Good dog.'

'Here we are.' Rob pulled the car into the kerb, and climbed out to help Sally unload. 'Carry that for you? You've got your hands full, what with him as well.'

'Oh.' It was a logical offer it would be illogical—it would be noticeable—to refuse. And she wished to draw no more attention to herself than she had already received from the populace of Stourhaven. 'Thank you,' she said, and let him take the holdall. 'Come on, Skipper—oh.'

Josephine was sitting on her pillar, her back all too pointedly turned as she stared in the opposite direction towards the house. In the fading light Skipper did not see her, but Sally had a shrewd suspicion she knew very well he

251

was near. Most cats would have wanted to know just who was arriving in a strange car right beside them: but not Josephine. Not when she had guessed, and was plainly furious about it. No front garden could be quite so fascinating.

The two of them would just have to learn to rub along together, Sally told herself.

Rob left the engine running as they walked through the gate and up the front path. Skipper growled at the rustle of Josephine's stalking passage through the bushes, but was otherwise quiet until they reached the door—

Where he exploded. As Sally produced her key he let out a volley of barks so loud she was almost deafened, and Rob was so unnerved he dropped the holdall. It landed with a thud and slipped from the step to the path. As he bent to pick it up, Sally struggled to open the door.

And struggle she did. Skipper was wild to get inside. For the first time she saw why the breed might be thought diabolic. One minute he was a fluffy little black dog: the next he was twice the size, a bristling sable whirlwind of barks and furious roars, impossible to control. The hard plastic of the expanding lead jerked from her startled hand as he plunged ahead of her into the house, sounding more like a pack of wolves in full cry than one small Schipperke.

There was a shout from indoors. Several shouts—yells—and screeches oddly tenor in tone. Either the Wellands had come home unexpectedly, or they—Sally—had burglars.

'Burglars!' Rob abandoned the holdall and prepared to charge to the rescue. 'You get the police!'

'Skipper!' cried Sally, but neither could hear the other above the noise of combat. Frantic footsteps pursued by barks approached the door at high speed. Sally found herself grabbing the holdall by the handles. Thrown hard it might take the wind from somebody's midriff sails—

'Gettim off! Gerroff, you little devil! Get out!' She had not yet positioned herself as two men in dark clothes erupted through the front door with Skipper at their heels, his nylon lead whipping behind, before, about him as he pranced and barked, roared and nipped at every reachable inch of the hapless intruders.

The cowards tried to lash out at him with their boots, but he was too quick. This time he had the advantage of surprise coupled with the power of a righteous indignation. His jaws snapped and worried at trousers and shoelaces. The flying plastic handle cracked on ankle-bones and shins. The men cursed—tripped—stumbled. Their hands shot out as they lost their balance, and as one of them fell Rob Halliday charged towards the other to finish with his fists what brave little Skipper had begun.

'Skipper!' Sally was terrified her dog would

be crushed in the fall, but as he fell the man must somehow have knocked the button that controlled the lead's mechanism. Black nylon cord tightened round a flailing human foot as black furred vengeance shot off to assist Rob with their second victim, but was brought up short with a jerk that had the first man, struggling to his feet, losing his balance again.

Sally gripped the holdall and tried to take aim. She hesitated. The two fighting men moved so fast she could not, in the twilight, be sure of her target. Skipper had obeyed his primaeval instincts and returned to the easier prey, leaping up and down on the chest of the fallen man and roaring in his face. The man screamed, and batted uselessly at the dog with his hands.

Sally followed Skipper's excellent example and went for the man on the ground: better to be sure of one than risk having both escape. With Skipper on his chest, the man's abdomen was worth a try. She flung the holdall with her whole strength and scored a direct hit. The man doubled up with a screech a tail-trapped cat could not have bettered, throwing Skipper off as he writhed and choked.

'Skipper!' But he could not hear her. His eyes were no longer blurred, brown, short-sighted—they glowed with a dull red fire as he prepared to launch himself again to the attack. Sally tried to seize his lead, but the nylon cord burned into her hands. The winded man's foot

254

knocked her glasses from her nose—

She was lost. Dimly, she could just make out two shapes she knew must be Rob and the second man, yet still she could not tell which was which. As she groped for her spectacles she saw a brutal fist crack on an unguarded jaw—one man stagger and fall—the other ready his boots for the kill—

And two more men burst from nowhere, sending Skipper's already frantic barks into a higher gear than she would have thought possible. She gave up all hope of controlling him, abandoned her glasses as a lost cause, and prepared to go down fighting, grabbing the holdall and ignoring the sharp pain as her burned palms closed about the handles. She took a deep breath—

And watched these men leap at the two men fighting and bring one crashing down with a neatness that spoke of practised teamwork. One man flipped him over, face into the earth, and wrenched his arms painfully up to his shoulder blades. The other—Sally braced herself—ignored both her and Skipper, bounding past them to apply the same painful manoeuvre to their gurgling captive . . .

The cavalry was here. Sally did not know— could not see—who these welcome newcomers were, but they were evidently not on the same side as the burglars. They wrestled their prisoners into submission, while by the light of the street-lamp Sally saw her glasses gleam and managed to get them back on her nose. They were dusty, scratched, but not broken: those plastic lenses had been worth every penny.

Now she could see what was going on.

Rob lay motionless on the ground. His assailant was a groaning bundle beneath the weight of a kneeling, stern-faced man in an anorak.

An anorak.

Two men.

The bird-watching train spotters from the station.

Sally looked at the second cavalry man. He, too, wore an anorak—and shoes with heavy soles . . .

But she was more bothered now about Skipper than explanations. He was still bouncing, barking, trying to bite: and she knew enough law to understand Reasonable Force. She knew too how fast the little dog could move if he did not mean to be caught. Rather than make the mistake of standing up and warning him she gave a sudden lunge forward, landing across the holdall, and flung out her hands to knock him over on his back before scooping him up to safety.

He yelped with surprise and indignation, kicking and thrashing with all four feet, trying to stop Sally clamping her hand over his muzzle. The lumpy contents of the holdall dug into her ribs. Skipper howled and yodelled.

Sally's breath came in gasps. With an effort she pushed herself more or less upright, kneeling with Skipper in her arms to survey the scene.

Rob was still motionless, his attacker still groaning. Sally's two rescuers looked at her in silence. Skipper gurgled in her arms. She could not speak.

She looked at the anorak men again. 'Thank you,' she said at last. They looked at her. They bowed.

'Thank you,' they said.

Or so at first she thought they said, above Skipper's continued yodels. But she must have misheard. Why should those who rescued her be thanking Sally Jackson?

Skipper went on howling through his nose. She knew she should get him inside—call the police . . .

She looked down at the holdall. Her hands were full with Skipper. Rob did not move.

The anorak men moved. They looked at each other; nodded. One of them put his hand in his pocket and produced a gun. He pointed it at Sally.

'Thank you,' he said again, and held out his hand.

257

CHAPTER TWENTY-FOUR

In moments of crisis, whose mind will work as clearly as it should? All Sally could do was stare, and clutch Skipper tightly. 'This—this isn't his real collar,' she brought out at last. 'He—he lost the other one.' Mrs Beeton would have come up with something far more heroic, but real life happens much faster than the plotting speed of mystery fiction.

'The bag,' said the man with the gun. 'You will allow my comrade to take it, you and your small dog who fights as a mountain lion. We wish you no harm. We wish only the bag. Thank you.'

Amazingly, he bowed again, although not so low that his eyes ever left watching her. Them. Skipper had not stopped his kicking and howling. If she let him go . . .

She could not let him go. He was still attached by his lead to the feet of the man he had tripped up however many hours ago that was. Nor could Sally herself move far without first releasing Skipper from his collar—and only a fool, or someone very sure of what she was doing, would try such tricks against a stern-faced man with a gun.

She gulped, and tried to summon the shade of Mrs Beeton for inspiration. 'It—it's not your bag,' she found herself saying. Of all the stupid things! 'It's—it's mine.' Accuracy somehow seemed terribly important: she had no idea why. 'The grey one, that is, not the g-green.'

'Ah,' said the man with the gun, giving a signal to his comrade colleague, who started walking towards Sally in a wide circle, keeping well out of the direct line of fire. '*Your* bag: a bourgeois concept. Property, so we read, is theft—and of theft your society must disapprove quite as strongly as ours. The bag may in truth be your property.' His voice was accusing. 'The contents of this bag, however, are not. You will be returned your bag when the contents are secured to us.'

Mrs Beeton would at this point have whipped her golden ladle from her pocket and started bopping heads until the forces of right should prevail; but Mrs Beeton would not have had both her hands fully occupied with thirteen pounds of indignant dog.

In a book or a film, Rob Halliday would have been only feigning unconsciousness until he could disarm the gunman and hold him and his colleague at bay ...

Real life was not like that.

There was nothing Sally could safely do or say, so like any sensible craven she did and said it. In silence she watched the gunman. In silence he watched Sally and Skipper, who was the only one of the little group making any noise. And that noise, substantial. In

259

(comparative) silence the comrade reached Sally and bent to pick up her battleship-grey holdall.

'Stop right there!'

It was an English voice, and male—but it was not Rob Halliday who spoke. Nor was it either of the burglars. Sally looked away from the comrade and the gunman to the end of the front garden, where several tall, looming figures had appeared in the pool of light from the street-lamp and were striding down the path in her direction . . .

She had never expected there would come a time when she was so glad to see Superintendent Groby.

*   *   *

'But how,' demanded Mrs Manchester, 'did the police arrive so quickly? I telephoned, of course, once I realised something was wrong, but I feel sure it can have been no more than a minute or two before they arrived.'

'It was the family at the station who raised the alarm,' Sally told her. 'When the Kovarians saw me leave in Rob's taxi they were afraid they'd lose sight of me altogether, so they pulled a gun on them just as they were getting into their car—it had taken them ages to sort themselves out because they kept dropping things—and they just hijacked it, and came chasing after us.' She knew there were far too many pronouns for absolute clarity, but her nerves had not yet recovered from their jangling of the previous night.

'It took them longer than they expected,' she went on, confident Mrs Manchester would take her meaning, 'because in Kovar they don't drive on the same side of the road as us, and they were apparently worried about being stopped by the police and never finding me again.'

'They could always have asked Rob Halliday where he had taken you.' Mrs Manchester frowned. 'That is, if there are taxis in Kovar— if they would understand the concept that they were likely to see him again.' She saw Sally's shocked expression. 'Oh, dear, how foolish of me,' she said softly. 'Poor young Halliday had been knocked unconscious by those two desperadoes who were raiding your house— not that the Kovarians would have known that, of course.' Now it was Mrs Manchester's turn to express shock. 'Oh, my dear Sally, you are so very lucky that they came when they did.'

Sally shuddered. 'You can say that again, though I was too busy being scared to realise it at the time—and trying to keep Skipper out of trouble, too. Oh, I know now that I wasn't in any danger from the Kovarians—they're a very law-abiding nation on the whole, but desperate causes need desperate remedies. That's why they hijacked the car and took the risk of driving without insurance or a licence. That's why,' she went on, as Mrs Manchester smiled, 'they were on the train in the first place. They weren't legally allowed to drive over here . . .'

Sally yawned, and found that the sudden influx of oxygen did wonders for her mental processes. 'And Terry Spernall couldn't drive at all. That was really the key, you might say, to the whole thing.'

'Ah,' breathed Mrs Manchester, leaning forward to fasten her bright eyes on Sally's rather weary ones. Last night had been yet another of those when her quality of sleep left much to be desired. 'Terry Spernall . . .'

'Went everywhere by public transport if he couldn't cadge a lift from someone, and he'd fallen out with most of his associates over the years. You name it, he travelled on it. Bus, train, cross-Channel ferry . . . He often popped across to the continent to—to dispose of certain items he might find an embarrassment over here . . .'

'Using the excuse of a visit to his cousins,' supplied Mrs Manchester, as Miss Jackson stifled another yawn. 'In Belgium, where as a child he first saw the Schipperke as a watchdog breed.' Obviously the Chattery had been chatting at full speed while Skipper and Sally were attempting to sleep off the effects of their adventure.

'Yes,' Sally said. 'He might have smuggled him in from abroad, but he didn't. Perhaps he had some cock-eyed logic that it wasn't right to break the law any more than he—well, than he had to for—for professional purposes.' Mrs Manchester suppressed a ladylike snort. Sally hurried on, 'The vet was furious with him for getting another dog when he'd already had two Alsatians and rehomed them—he said they ate too much, and were a nuisance when he left them, and his mother couldn't cope with them. Skipper was a more handy size to leave with her when he went away.'

'Which he finally did about a year ago,' Mrs Manchester reminded her. 'Never to be seen in Stourhaven again—with the result that her solicitors had to advertise for him when his poor mother died.' She twinkled at Sally. 'Should one now hazard the conjecture that there is indeed a connection of some sort between this melancholy occurrence and the stirring events of more recent days?'

'Oh, yes. Everyone thought they'd quarrelled. Perhaps they had, and she threw him out—he was hardly a likeable character— but he had his reasons, in a warped sort of way. You see, a year ago he went to Belgium for—for the usual purposes, and while he was there he heard about the Artansky exhibition across the border in Beneluxia.'

'Artansky.' Mrs Manchester pursed her lips. 'The name is familiar, in a vaguely . . . expensive way. Let me think. Artansky . . .' After a moment or two, she smiled. 'Being housebound has its advantages, my dear,

263

provided one has not lost one's faculties. I read a most interesting history of the Russian Imperial Court only the other week, in which there was some mention of Fabergé and the extravagant pieces of jewellery he fashioned for Tsarina Alexandra at the request of her husband Nicholas. Was a Germanius Artansky at one time not a pupil of Fabergé?'

'That's the man. He was a Beneluxian who wanted to see the world and make money, and who succeeded in doing both. When the Conif of Kovar decided to have the Crown Regalia reworked in a style more in keeping with his—his aspirations, Artansky did a splendid job and charged the absolute earth—and got it. Of course the Conif was a very wealthy man, but even if he hadn't been he would have thought it beneath his royal dignity to quibble at the price.'

'Unlike some,' interposed Mrs Manchester, with a shrewd look at Sally.

'Exactly.' She suspected Mrs Manchester already knew what she would say next, but carried on regardless. 'Artansky was so used to penny-pinching monarchs that when he came across one who just signed the cheques, or whatever they did in those days, he went around singing the chap's praises and vowing eternal friendship. Which came in jolly useful for the Conif and his family when the Kovarians launched their own revolution a few years after the Russians in 1917.'

'Beneluxia accepted the deposed Kovarian court as refugees,' Mrs Manchester said. Sally knew she had known all along. 'Artansky was the country's most famous citizen, and it was considered that the honours were equal on both sides when the Conif and his family chose to settle there. Didn't one of the young Coniffas marry an Artansky relative?'

The potted history of the Kovarian People's glorious Republic (formerly the Imperial Kingdom of Kovar) to which Sally had listened last night had omitted that particular point. 'She may have done,' said Sally. 'It would make sense. Many Beneluxians can claim aristocratic or royal Kovarian descent, and with the collapse of Communism the ties between the two countries are even stronger than they were. When Kovar decided to make a real play for western sympathies, it agreed to lend the Regalia to Beneluxia when there was a centenary exhibition of Artansky's work— and Terry Spernall heard about it.'

Sally paused. 'Beneluxia isn't a large country. Not very—not very sophisticated.'

'Ruritanian,' suggested Mrs Manchester.

Sally nodded. 'Their security isn't at all what it should be—or it wasn't, a year ago.' She grimaced. 'It's red hot now, I should imagine.' A sad loss of innocence—or a belated acceptance of the real world? 'They had the whole Imperial Kovarian Regalia there, on loan from the Kovar State Museum—and

265

Terry Spernall popped across from Belgium, and pinched it.'

CHAPTER TWENTY-FIVE

Officially she had not been there. Superintendent Groby made this very clear to Sally. She had done no more than accompany him to the police station to lodge a formal complaint against the burglars whose felonious activities her homecoming had interrupted. The anorak-wearing strangers who had so unexpectedly rushed to her rescue during the aftermath of that interruption must be questioned about the legality of the firearm more than one witness had seen in their possession—and if she happened to be in the background, waiting to read and sign the typed copy of her verbal statement, an overworked detective might well be forgiven for having failed to notice someone as small and unimportant as Sally M. Jackson.

A failure to notice Skipper would have been more unforgivable—but Skipper was not there. Given the unusual size of the suspect bag and the limited number of interview rooms, Sergeant Biggin had for the second week running been dragged from his cosy Sunday evening *en famille* to keep an eye on everyone. The sergeant, past master at delegation, had on this occasion quickly rounded up enough uniformed constables to make his presence purely supervisory, taking the little dog under his benevolent wing in lieu of the spaniel waiting for him at home in front of the television. The last Sally had seen of the hero of the hour he was being patted by about six people at once, and licking digestive biscuit crumbs from (she was thankful to see) the end of the packet. She did not want him back at the vet's on Monday with an upset inside.

The rescuing anoraks, gunman and comrade, had obediently raised their hands the instant Superintendent Groby identified himself as a police officer. As Sally would later say to Mrs Manchester, the Kovarians were a law-abiding nation. Even their Glorious Revolution had only deposed, rather than executed, their imperial family; and they were never such extremists that they demolished palaces, burned decadent books and paintings, or melted down jewels and gold for use as hard currency.

'I most greatly regret,' said the one Kovarian who could speak English, 'the necessity for force.' He contrived to bow, even while remaining seated. 'But our enquiries, and those of our comrades in Beneluxia, had shown that this man Spernall was a rough customer indeed.' He looked proud at his grasp of colloquialism, and Sally smiled. Superintendent Groby muttered something under his breath.

'We could not but suppose,' the Kovarian continued, 'his comrades would be just so rough as he, and therefore took appropriate safeguards for our protection as we pursued his trail.' He sighed. 'The Preventive officer who examined us when our vessel first reached these waters was not, I fear, told the entire truth, but any delay might have seriously impeded our search. Had we been able to claim diplomatic immunity—'

'I don't think we want to hear about that,' broke in Groby with a shudder. Telephone wires had hummed between Stourhaven and whichever Foreign Office mandarin the F.O.'s weekend emergency desk had managed to unearth. Sally had not been present for the discussion, but the general import was obvious: sort it all out with the minimum of fuss.

'So,' prompted Groby, as the Kovarian (whose name, though four times repeated, nobody could pronounce) allowed himself a scornful arch of the eyebrow at this evidence of bourgeois duplicity. 'So you came to England—to Stourhaven—after someone tipped you off that Terry Spernall was responsible for the theft of the Crown Jewels from the exhibition?'

The Kovarian nodded. 'There are many sympathisers to our cause in the kingdom of Beneluxia, also many who regard it as an insult to the honour of their country that such a theft should have been perpetrated in the capital city. We had much to avenge, Comrade Superintendent, on behalf of others beside ourselves.'

'Yes, and I'd rather not hear about vengeance, either.' Groby picked up the gun, from which the bullets had been extracted, and turned it over in his hands. 'I ought to impound this, you know.'

The Kovarian shrugged. 'It matters nothing, now our task is successfully performed. We have our crown regalia once more . . .'

All eyes turned to the table in the middle of the room. On their newspaper carpet, gleaming richly under a harsh electric light, lay the Ceremonial Chain, the Coronation Orb, and the Crown of the former Imperial Kingdom of Kovar. And what a crown it was. No mere diadem, tiara or humble coronet, it was a massive circlet of wrought gold with four proud arches soaring, gem-encrusted, over a cap of crimson velvet to a larger version of that strange double-barred cross, on top of which a solitary diamond was set in eight golden claws shaped like the feet of lions.

'. . . and you, as I understand,' continued the Kovarian, 'have your murderer.'

Groby, who had been about to protest, did not. A faint smile twisted the lips of the Kovarian. He glanced at his silent compatriot, and said something in a language that evidently preferred consonants to vowels. The silent one smiled, too. Groby winced.

'Two men are helping us with our enquiries,' he said at last. 'They're innocent until proved guilty, of course.'

'Of course.' Another seated bow, tinged with irony. 'One must await the trial, and the verdict. Yet could it not be said,' with a deeper bow for Sally, 'that verdict has already been pronounced in the person of one small dog?'

Groby shuddered, and glared in Sally's direction, though she had said nothing. 'The dog seems friendly enough, on the whole,' he conceded. 'As dogs go. But you're seriously trying to tell me it—it recognised those two as the ones who had knifed its master? I don't know how well that would stand up in court. The men were burglars, for pity's sake. Trespassing. You'd expect a dog to have a go at them.'

'Were not I and my comrade likewise trespassers? Also the—the chauffeur.' He frowned. 'The driver of the car one may engage on a temporary basis.'

'Taxi driver,' supplied Sally, as Groby snorted. 'Or cabbie, if you prefer a more colloquial term.'

'Cabbie. Thank you.' The Kovarian smiled and nodded. 'This cabbie, then, while in your employ might have been understood by your dog to have legitimate cause on your property. To contrast we, of a certainty, had none. Yet it was not at any time towards us that his anger was directed, even when . . .'

'When you pulled a gun on me to take the holdall.' Sally glanced at the superintendent, who was staring straight at the opposite wall, his shoulders rigid. 'He wasn't happy, though,' she reminded the gunman. 'I couldn't say for sure he wouldn't have gone for you as well, if he'd been able.'

'Oh, this your scientists will prove,' the Kovarian said, with an easy confidence in the forensic prowess of the west. 'And your London police. The man Spernall was stabbed. We will learn that the knife was property of these burglars, one or other. Their names will be placed into the computer and found to be associates—unless this has already been done,' he added, as Groby twitched on his chair, and his shoulders jerked. 'Yes?'

'I'm saying nothing,' said the superintendent. 'But—well—Sunday evening's not a good time to get mugshots identified, but if there just so happens to be a bloke on duty at the Yard who might recognise a couple of faces from the not-too-distant past, I'm not saying it isn't possible to have a good idea who used to pal around with who, until they fell out.'

The Kovarian digested this in silence. Again he nodded. 'The men . . . fell out. And were afterwards in pursuit—as we, also. Questions must be asked, without arousing suspicion.' Sally remembered the harbour master, but kept quiet. 'Answers must be . . . . followed.

271

Confirmed. It was in London we had some intimation that what we sought, and these men, might not be utterly beyond recall: and then we saw you, Miss Jackson, and your little dog. You were not entirely unrecognised by us, with what you carried . . .'

Regular users of public transport are far more likely to think of Left Luggage than those who travel mostly by car. What had finally prompted Terry's two former friends—whose interest in making a quick profit had been awakened by his celebratory ramblings over more than a few drinks on his safe return from Beneluxia—to think of searching Sally's house a second time, for something far smaller than the contents of the olive-green holdall, could only be guessed . . .

It was a week later that Sally had learned how Terry hid his Kovarian loot in a Beneluxian Left Luggage locker and, with his ticket expiring at the end of twelve months, went back to retrieve the holdall once the hue and cry had died down. But before he could carry out his plans to turn the imperial regalia into cash, the notice from his mother's solicitor came to his attention. It would take time to arrange for a fence. Inheritance was straightforward and immediate. On that momentous Thursday he stashed the holdall at Waterling Cross, clipped the key on Skipper's collar, bought a ticket to Stourhaven . . .

'They grabbed him just outside the station.'

Sergeant Biggin eased himself into a more comfortable slump on the five-barred gate. 'Then they took him for a little walk to—to chat about things. And you know what happened next, Miss Jackson.'

Sally shivered, and pulled at Skipper's ears for reassurance; whether his or hers, she did not know. 'Yes,' she said. 'And the time factor suggests he must have come down from London on the train before mine. Ugh.'

'The key of his mother's house was in his pocket. He'd obviously planned to spend the night there before dropping into the solicitors next day—and the two who did for him missed out on the chance to search him because he got away from them in the dark.'

'And I raised the alarm.'

'And heard what he said,' the sergeant reminded her. 'Not as they knew he'd said anything, to begin with. But they had the feeling if they hung around long enough they'd find out something to their advantage, and with their contact at the solicitor's office . . .'

Sally looked surprised, although a moment's thought told her she should have wondered earlier how the two from London had known when to leave town and set up the ambush in Stourhaven.

'Terry Spernall had a lot of people . . . interested in a little chat,' explained the sergeant, chewing on a pensive blade of grass, 'if he stayed in one place long enough for them to find him. He'd dropped right out of sight over the past year, and there was a fair bit of unfinished business here as well as in Town.' He coughed. 'When two London toughs turned up here asking questions it wasn't hard for 'em to persuade the local talent to join forces. One lad has a brother with a girlfriend who's a typist, see, at the solicitors. So our lot told the townies Terry would likely soon be on his way, but they didn't have the wit to think of a double-cross, or how there might be more to it than they'd been told. Stolen crown jewels is way out of the Stourhaven league: we're more for the quiet life here. A bit of smuggling. Creeping about in the dark . . .'

Sally jumped. 'They were keeping an eye on me all the time!' she cried. 'I kept getting a—a creepy sort of feeling somebody was watching me, but I thought it was my imagination. Nerves.'

'Which wouldn't have been a surprise, considering.' The sergeant smiled. 'Mind you, much of the time I'd have to say it was nerves, once our local lot had decided you were nothing to do with Terry Spernall, which anyone taking the trouble to talk to you could've told. But these Londoners, they don't take the word of a bunch of hayseeds. They were sure Terry must've somehow got the stuff to his girlfriend without them knowing, so they searched your house—and you'd not got it . . .'

Girlfriend?

Was the reputation of Sally M. Jackson, creator of that long-established crimebuster Mrs Beeton, sufficient to withstand the charge of being a gangster's moll?

CHAPTER TWENTY-SIX

In the pages of crime fiction life is often awkward for the innocent bystander. Sally's involvement in the murder of Terry Spernall had undoubtedly been innocent; and her life had had more than its share of awkwardness since she opened her front door to find a dying man on the step.

Life had its benefits, too. She tugged Skipper's soft black ears again, and he licked her hand. Beside the pair a plump and stately spaniel snuffled in the grass.

'Nice little dog,' observed Sergeant Biggin, amiably nodding in Skipper's direction. 'There'll be no mention in the files, o' course. Some of these hoodlums, they start bleating about unfair provocation and showing their bites and bruises, and the next thing you know there's a vet with a needle and a nasty look in his eye. But we've evidence enough without his lordship there,' he said, as Sally stared at him in horror. He winked. 'Imagination, we'll call it if they say anything. Or nerves. Or else those foreign friends of yours, off home now where we can't get at them, rabies laws or not.'

Sally sighed with relief. She was more than happy to accept the public theory of quarantine-ignorant Kovarians having brought a tracker dog with them; and yet it saddened her that Skipper could not receive due credit for his undoubted courage on the night of the burglary . . . and before, when he had defended Terry Spernall in the woodland dark and been close to death himself.

But better safe than sorry. 'Even diplomatic immunity,' she agreed, 'wouldn't protect a dog from the rabies laws if they hadn't got the vaccination paperwork. No wonder they went off in such a hurry once they had the regalia back.'

'No wonder, indeed.' Sergeant Biggin had, like Sally, wangled a closer look at the contents of the olive-green bag before they and it were handed back by Superintendent Groby to the English-speaking Kovarian and his comrade. There had been some dispute over the value of photographs as evidence, settled in the superintendent's favour by the production of a Polaroid camera. Diplomatic relations were not, however, so relaxed that Groby would consent to the swap tentatively proposed. If the Kovarians wanted an instant camera, they must acquire it in the usual capitalist way. 'Just as well,' said Sergeant Biggin now, 'Terry didn't get away with more, or we'd never have sorted it all out.'

Sally thought it would take a crook with more cunning than Terry Spernall, as well as catastrophically slack Beneluxian security, for him to have walked off with the sceptres, the sword and the scabbard as well as the crown, the orb, and the ceremonial chain of the People's Republic of Kovar: but she agreed with Sergeant Biggin. How much more eventful would her life have been of late if there had been not one, but two holdalls worth more than double the value of one?

Not that she had had time to consider this point at the time she first spoke to Mrs Manchester. She and Sergeant Biggin had yet to bump into each other while out walking their dogs the following Sunday afternoon, and to enjoy their most illuminating chat. That previous Sunday night (or rather Monday morning) when Superintendent Groby at last agreed Sally and Skipper could go home, and would Sergeant Biggin sort something out, the sergeant had sorted to excellent effect. The uniformed driver was the cheery young man with the moustache, who accompanied Sally right up her front path, waited politely while Skipper anointed the requisite number of bushes, and checked the house thoroughly before allowing them inside. The emergency glazier had already been and gone. All was well.

'And Sergeant Biggin says, Miss Jackson, that you want to take good care of your little dog here. A regular hero, he is.' The honest eyes above the regulation shirt shone clear and bright. 'Plenty of fresh air and exercise, he says. Like he gives his on Sundays. Always takes a walk round the golf course Sundays, does Sergeant Biggin. Says it helps his digestion after dinner.' Which Sally knew meant lunch. 'Never misses, he doesn't, whatever the weather.' And one honest eye closed in an unmistakeable wink.

'Oh,' said Sally. 'Yes. Please thank Sergeant Biggin. He's right. Skipper is a hero. He deserves the best. I'll follow the sergeant's advice to the letter, tell him.'

'Right you are,' said the moustache, with another wink, and a final pat for the hero bobbing and sniffing about his ankles. 'You remember, now!'

She did.

But she told Mrs Manchester little more than she had told her that first Monday. While she believed she now knew the full story, she felt Superintendent Groby would not approve of her knowing. Sergeant Biggin had trusted Sally Jackson to keep her own counsel: and, on the whole, she did.

She did not, however, think it any betrayal of that trust to tell her neighbour why Rob Halliday, now in hospital with concussion, had shown such interest in her affairs over the past week or so. While the Kovarians and her burglars were being loaded into police vehicles, Sally had gone to offer what first-aid assistance she could to the constable bending over the taxi driver's still unconscious form.

'He's breathing okay,' she was told, 'and I've put him in the recovery position while we wait for the ambulance. The bloody fool!' he added. 'I undid his shirt to listen to his heart, and . . .'

Although Rob lay on his side with his arm up and one knee bent, it was just possible to make out the tattoo beneath his left breast, and the pendant strung on a leather thong around his neck. The tattoo in an unprintable form, and the pendant in the shape of a five-pointed star . . .

'Witchcraft!' Mrs Manchester pursed her lips into a moue of distaste. 'Really, I would have thought better—even of a Halliday.'

'I don't know whether Ernie was involved or not, though if you ask me he was too busy gloating over the profits from renting out the Wellands' boat to all and sundry.' It was no wonder Ernie had accused Sally of nosy-parkering when she wanted to know if the boat was still in his safekeeping. That it was not had been yet another fact unearthed by the diligent Groby and his cohorts. 'Rob, on the other hand, seems to have been a—a biggish sort of bug in the group,' said Sally. 'Chief warlock, or some such nonsense.'

'Dancing naked around bonfires on lonely islands at midnight, no doubt,' said Mrs

Manchester, with a sniff. Sally nodded. It must have been Rob, warned by his brother, who had kept watch from the wooded bank to find out what she was doing, that day on Middle Eyot . . .

She—and Skipper. She shuddered. 'Once he found out the Schipperke is often called the Little Black Devil . . .'

But even in Mrs Manchester's quiet house she did not care to finish the thought. Who knew how warped the narrow minds of Stourhaven might yet be?

It had come as no surprise to Mrs Manchester that her new neighbour was making plans to leave the seaside town. Sally had tried for a week, but there was to be no stiff upper lip and face-the-blighters-down for one with her imagination on overdrive, and accelerating. She felt uneasy in the house after all that had happened: and with all that superstition told her still might. Her American colleague was finding it convenient to live near London, but rather more dull than she had anticipated. Sally would welcome a little dullness: her colleague would welcome Sally's company for a few days, or weeks, or months, as she chose, provided Sally did not interfere with her work, as she engaged not to interfere with Sally's.

The only other condition was that Sally must relate every detail of those recent adventures at which the media had only hinted . . .

This last condition was at first the most difficult to keep, until suddenly it became the easiest. Sally saw that with a few judicious name changes her adventure had the makings of a mystery—though not for Mrs Beeton. It was hard to imagine the travelling cook-housekeeper with a dog as well as a gold-plated ladle. Sally would find a new protagonist, and see how she liked her by the end of the book. If it was published she would send a signed copy to the old lady she had already rechristened Regina Manchester. Sally could imagine how thrilled she would be to receive the parcel in the post and learn the truth . . .

Sally's own parcel thrill arrived two days before she was due to leave Stourhaven. Skipper was helping her pack by climbing into each cardboard carton as she unfolded it, and trying to pretend he was a reference book. His pretence did not fool his mistress.

He startled her, however, when the doorbell rang. She had yet to grow used to the way he would leap up from whatever he was doing to gallop to the front of the house and hurl threats through the woodwork at whoever was outside.

Sally hurried after him, scooped him up, and opened the door—to have the postman hand her a small package covered in rough brown paper, bearing stamps of a design she had never seen before.

'Sorry to bother you,' said the postman, as Skipper gave him a very sharp look. 'I know it'd go through the letter-box okay, but I was wondering if you collected stamps. My boy does, see, and if you didn't want them he'd be glad of these for his album, I'm sure.'

'Hang on,' said Sally, and closed the door on him while she hurried to the kitchen for scissors. A few snips, and the stamps—was that Cyrillic script?—were his, with the requisite quarter-inch margin of paper left around them.

There was no return address on the parcel, but somehow she knew its contents were no great danger. She opened it, and found two flat, red leather boxes, one square and one oblong. She opened the square one first.

Nestling in crimson velvet she found an ornately-worked brooch in what looked like—what was—gold, decorated with florid curlicues and flashing gemstones she felt sure must be rubies and diamonds. There was a small square of white cardboard tucked under the clasp of the brooch. She pulled it out to read the fine, flowing script.

Thank you. That was all.

She opened the oblong box. She saw a gold chain, narrow, finely worked, and with a strange clasp that looked like—that, as Sally lifted it out, was—a buckle. Just like the buckle on a dog collar. Underneath the buckle, hanging from a golden ring, a miniature

282

medallion, oval in shape, embossed with the form of a lion, circled with tiny gems and heavy enough to be of solid gold.

In this box there was another white card. She pulled it out. The script, equally fine and flowing, was clear.

Hero of the Kovarian Republic, First Class.

'There!' said Sally, giving Skipper a proud, delighted cuddle. 'Now at least *someone* appreciates what a very brave dog you are!'

He flicked his ears at her.

We hope you have enjoyed this Large Print book. Other Chivers Press or Thorndike Press Large Print books are available at your library or directly from the publishers.

For more information about current and forthcoming titles, please call or write, without obligation, to:

Chivers Press Limited
Windsor Bridge Road
Bath BA2 3AX
England
Tel. (01225) 335336

OR

G.K. Hall & Co.
295 Kennedy Memorial Drive
Waterville
Maine 04901
USA

All our Large Print titles are designed for easy reading, and all our books are made to last.